I0749283

THE MOTOR GIRLS ON A TOUR

Margaret Penrose

The Motor Girls on a Tour

Margaret Penrose

PO Box 2211
Fairfield, IA 52556
www.1stworldlibrary.org
First Edition

LCCN: 2005906534

Softcover ISBN: 1-4218-1590-7
Hardcover ISBN: 1-4218-1490-0
eBook ISBN: 1-4218-1690-3

Purchase *"The Motor Girls on a Tour"*
as a traditional bound book at:
www.1stWorldLibrary.org/purchase.asp?ISBN=1-4218-1590-7

1st World Library Literary Society is a nonprofit organization dedicated to promoting literacy by:

- Creating a free internet library accessible from any computer worldwide.
- Hosting writing competitions and offering book publishing scholarships.

The Motor Girls on a Tour

contributed by Tim, Ed & Rodney
in support of
1st World Library Literary Society

CONTENTS

CHAPTER I

A SPOILED DINNER

The big maroon car glided along in such perfect rhythm that Cora Kimball, the fair driver of the Whirlwind, heard scarcely a sound of its mechanical workings. To her the car went noiselessly - the perfection of its motion was akin to the very music of silence.

Hazel Hastings was simply sumptuous in the tonneau - she had spread every available frill and flounce, but there was still plenty of unoccupied space on the luxuriously cushioned "throne."

It seemed a pity to passers-by that two girls should ride alone on that splendid morning in the handsome machine - so many of those afoot would have been glad of a chance to occupy the empty seats.

Directly following the Whirlwind came another car - the little silver Flyaway. In this also were two girls, the Robinson twins, Elizabeth and Isabel, otherwise Belle and Bess. Chelton folks were becoming accustomed to the sight of these girls in their cars, and a run of the motor girls was now looked upon as a daily occurrence. Bess Robinson guided her car with unmistakable skill - Cora Kimball was considered an expert driver.

Sputtering and chugging close to the Flyaway came a second

runabout. In this were a girl and a boy, or, more properly speaking, a young lady and a young gentleman. As they neared the motor girls Bess called back to Belle:

"There come Sid and Ida. I thought they were not on speaking terms."

"They were not, but they are now," answered Belle with a light laugh. "Why should a girl turn her back on a young man with a brand new machine?"

"It runs like a locomotive," murmured Bess, as, at that moment, the other car shot by, the occupants bowing indifferently to the Robinson girls as the machines came abreast.

Cora turned and shook her head significantly when the third car had forged ahead. She, too, seemed surprised that Ida Giles should be riding with Sid Wilcox. Then Bess rolled up alongside the Whirlwiind.

"My, but they are going!" she called to Cora. "I thought Ida said she would never ride with Sid again."

"Why not?" flashed Cora merrily. "Isn't Sid's car new and - yellow?"

"Like a dandelion," put in Belle, who was noted for her aesthetic tendencies. "And, precisely like a dandelion, I fancy that machine would collapse without rhyme or reason. Did you every try a bunch of dandelions on the table?"

The girls all laughed. No one but Belle Robinson would ever try such an experiment. Everybody knew the ingratitude of the yellow field flower.

"I can never bear anything of that color since my valentine luncheon," declared Belle bravely. "That's why I predict disaster for Sid's new car."

"They have dropped something!" exclaimed Hazel as she peered ahead at the disappearing runabout.

Bess had taken the lead.

"Let's put on speed," she suggested, and, pulling the lever, her car shot ahead, and was soon within close range of the yellow runabout.

"Be careful!" called her sister. "You will run over -"

It was too late. At that moment the Flyaway dashed over something - the pieces flew in all directions.

"Their lunch-hamper!" exclaimed Belle.

The runabout had turned to one side, and then stopped. Bess jammed on the brakes and also came to a standstill.

"Well!" growled Sid Wilcox, approaching the wreck in the road.

"I - couldn't stop," faltered Bess remorsefully.

"I guess you didn't try," snapped Ida Giles, her cheeks aflame almost to the tint of her fiery tresses.

"I really did," declared Bess. "I would not have spoiled your hamper for anything."

"And your lunch was in it?" gasped Belle. "We're awfully sorry!"

Bent and crippled enameled dishes from the lately fine and completely equipped auto-hamper were scattered about in all directions. Here and there a piece of pie could be identified, while the chicken sandwiches were mostly recognizable by the fact that a newly arrived yellow dog persistently gnawed at one or two particular mud spots.

"Oh, we can go to a hotel for dinner," announced the young man, getting back into his car.

"But they ought to pay for the hamper," grumbled Ida, loud enough for the Robinson girls to make sure of her remark.

"We will, of course," called Bess, just as Cora and Hazel came up, and then the Wilcox runabout darted off again.

"Table d'hote?" called Cora, laughing.

"No, a la carte," replied Bess, picking up a piece of damaged celery, putting it on a slice of uninjured bread and proffering it to Hazel.

"What a shame!" sighed Hazel. "Their picnic will be spoiled."

"But look at the picnic we've had," put in Belle. "You should have seen Ida's face. A veritable fireless cooker."

"And Sid - he supplied the salt hay," declared Bess. "I felt as if I were smothered in a ton of it."

"And that was the peace-offering hamper," declared Cora, alighting from her car and closely viewing the wreck. "Jack told me that Ida gave Sid a handsome hamper for the new car."

"I told you that the yellow machine would turn -"

"Dandelion," Hazel interrupted Belle. "Well, I agree with you that was an ungrateful trick. To demolish the lunch, of all other available things to do, on a day like this!"

"Souvenirs?" suggested Cora, removing her glove to dig out of the mud a knife, and then a fork.

"Oh, forget it!" exclaimed Bess. "I am sure I want to. Let's get going again, if we are to make the Woodbine Way in time to plan the tour. I'm just crazy about the trip," and the enthusiastic girl expended some of her pent-up energies on the crank at the front of the Flyaway.

Cora was also cranking up. "Yes," she said, "we had best be on the road again. We are due at the park at twelve. I expect Maud will have the family tree along and urge us to stop overnight at every gnarl on the `trunk.'"

"We might have asked Ida and Sid," reflected Belle aloud, sympathetically.

"Yes," Bess almost shouted, "and have them veto every single plan. Besides, there are to be no boys on this trip; Lady Isabel please take notice!"

"As if I wanted boys!" sneered her sister.

"As if you could have them if you did!" fired back Bess in that tantalizing way that only sisters understand, only sisters enjoy, and only sisters know how to operate successfully.

"Peace! peace!" called Cora. "If Belle wants boys she may have them. I am chairman of the acting committee, and if boys do not act I would like to know exactly what they do."

"No boys!" faltered Hazel, who, not owning a machine, had not as yet heard all the details of the proposed three-days' tour of the motor girls.

"Nary a one!" returned Bess, now about to start.

"If we had boys along," explained Cora, "they would claim the glory of every spill, every skid, every upset and every `busted tire.' We want some little glory ourselves," and at this she threw in the clutch, and, with a gentle effort, the Whirlwind rolled off, followed closely by the Flyaway.

"I suppose Sid and Ida are licking their fingers just about

now," remarked the good-natured Bess.

"Very likely," rejoined her sister, "for I fancv their meal was made up of buckwheat cakes and molasses, as Sid had to pay for it."

"Oh, I meant sheer deliciousness," corrected her sister. "I 'fawncy'" - and she imitated the dainty tones used by Belle - "they have had -"

"Backbiting and detraction," called Cora, who had been close enough to hear the sisters' remarks. "I would not have been in your place at that table, Bess, for a great deal."

Bess tossed her head about indifferently. She evidently knew what to expect from Ida and Sid.

"Now for a straight run!" announced Cora, throwing in third speed. "We must make the bridge by the quarter whistle or the Maud Morris family tree may have been consumed for luncheon. I particularly want a peg at that tree."

"We're off!" called Bess, following with additional speed.

Then the Whirlwind and the Flyaway dashed off, over the country roads, past scurrying chicks and barking dogs, past old farmers who turned in to give "them blamed things" plenty of room, out along Woodbine to the pretty little park where the plans for the first official run of the motor girls were soon to be perfected.

CHAPTER II

THE WOODLAND CONFERENCE

In the first volume of this series, entitled "The Motor Girls; Or, A Mystery of the Road," we became acquainted with these vivacious young ladies. Cora Kimball, the first to own her own motor-car, the Whirlwind, was the only daughter of Mrs. Grace Kimball, a wealthy widow of the little town of Chelton. Jack Kimball, Cora's brother, a typical college boy, had plenty to do in unraveling the mystery of the road, while his chums, Walter Pennington and Edward Foster, were each such attractive young men that even to the end it was difficult to guess which one would carry off the highest honors socially - with Cora as judge, of course.

It was Ed Foster who lost the money, a small fortune, and it was the rather unpleasant Sid Wilcox, and perhaps unfortunate Ida Giles, who finally cleared up the mystery, happily enough, all things considered, although in spite of the other girls' opportune intention it was not possible to reflect any degree of credit upon those responsible for the troubles and trials which that mystery involved.

Speaking of the young men, Paul Hastings, a young chauffeur, should not be overlooked. Paul was a very agreeable youth indeed, and his sister, Hazel, a most interesting young lady, with very special qualities of talent and learning.

"Among those present" in the first volume were the attractive

Robinson twins, Bess inclined to rather more weight than height, and Belle, the tall, graceful creature, who delighted in the aesthetic and reveled in "nerves."

Mr. Perry Robinson, the girls' father, was a wealthy railroad magnate, devoted to carriage rides, and not caring for motors, but not too "set" to allow his daughters the entire ownership of the pretty new runabout - the Flyaway.

Cora, Hazel, Bess and Belle were flying over the country roads in their cars, making for Woodbine Park, where they were to hold a preliminary meet to arrange for a tour on the road.

Past the bridge at the appointed time, they reached the wooded park exactly at twelve - the hour set for the rest and luncheon, to be followed by the "business meeting."

"There come Daisy and Maud," called Cora, as along the winding road she discerned another car approaching.

"And there are Clip and Ray," added Belle, shutting off the gasoline and preparing to bring her machine to a standstill.

"I think it a shame to call Cecilia Thayer Clip," objected Belle. "She is no more of a romp than -"

"Any boy," interrupted Bess. "Well, the boys call her Clip, and it's handy."

By this time the new car was up in line with the others.

"'Lo, there!" called Cecilia, jerking her machine to a stop in the manner deplored by skilled mechanicians.

"Look out!" cautioned Cora. "You'll `bust' something."

Cecilia had bounded out on the road.

"Stiff as a stick!" she exclaimed with a rather becoming twist of her agile form. "I never make that road without absorbing every bump on the thoroughfare."

Cecilia was not altogether pretty, for she had the "accent on her nose," as Cora put it, but she was dashing, and, at a glance, one might easily guess why she had been called Clip.

Rachel Stuart was a striking blonde, tall to a fault, pink and white to bisqueness and, withal, evidently conscious of her charms. Even while motoring she affected the pastel tints, and this morning looked radiant in her immense blue scarf and her well-matched blue linen coat.

"You look," said Cora to Cecilia, as the latter continued to shake herself out of the absorbed bumps, "like nothing so much as like a `strained' nurse - Jack's variety."

"Exactly that!" admitted Cecilia. "I have been searching high and low for a cheap and economical rig to drive in, and I have just hit upon this." She pirouetted wonderfully. "All ready made -the `strained' nurse variety, sure enough. How do you like it?"

"Very becoming," decided Bess.

"And very practical," announced Belle.

"Sweet," declared Cora.

"When you say a good thing, stop," ordered Cecilia, just as Ray was about to give her verdict.

"And now to the woods," suggested Cora. "We may as well put our machines up in the open near the grove. We can see them there, and make sure that no one is tempted to investigate them."

It was a level stretch over the field to the grove. Cora led the way and the others followed. Lunch baskets and boxes were quickly gathered up from the machines, and, with the keenness of appetite common to young and healthy, and "painful" to our fair motorists (for Cecilia declared her appetite "hurt"), the party scampered off to an appropriate spot where the lunch might be enjoyed.

"And there are to be no boys?" asked Maud Morris, she with the "imploring look," as Cecilia put it, although Maud was familiarly known as a very sweet girl.

"No boys!" echoed Bess, between uncertain mouthfuls.

Daisy Bennet turned her head away in evident disapproval.

"No boys," she repeated faintly. Daisy did everything faintly. She was a perfectly healthy young girl, but a little affected otherwise - too fond of paper-covered books, and perhaps too fond of other sorts of romance. But we must not condemn Daisy - her mother had the health-traveling habit, and what was Daisy to do with herself?

Cora handed around some lettuce sandwiches.

"I am just as keen on boys as any of you," she admitted, "but for a real motor girl tour it is apparent that boys will have to be tabooed."

Bess grunted, Belle sighed, Cecilia bit her tongue, Ray raised her eyebrows, Hazel made a "minute" of the report.

"And silence ensued," commented Cecilia, reaching back of Maud and securing a dainty morsel from the lunch-box of the latter.

"Water?" called Bess.

"Yes," chimed in Cecilia, "go and fetch some."

"The spring is away down the other side of the hill,"

objected Bess.

"You need the exercise," declared Cecilia.

"Clip, you go fetch some," suggested Cora, "and I'll give you half my pie."

Without another word Clip was on her feet, had upset Daisy's improvised table of sticks and paper napkins in her haste to secure the water bottle, and was now running over the hill toward the spring.

Presently she stopped as if listening to something. Then she turned and hurried back to the party on the grass. Her face was white with alarm.

"Oh!" she gasped. "I heard the awfullest groans! Some one must be either dying for a drink, or dying from a drink. The groans were wet!"

Cora jumped up, as did some of the others.

"Come on," said Cora. "I'm not afraid. Some one may need help."

"Oh, they do - I am sure," panted Cecilia. "All kinds of help, I should say. The moans were chromatic."

"Listen!" commanded Cora, as the sounds came over the hill. Low, then fierce growls and groans, tapering down to grunts and exclamation marks sounded through the grove.

"Oh!" screamed Belle.

"What can it be?" exclaimed Daisy.

"Almost anything," suggested Cora. "But we had best be specific," and she started in the direction of the mysterious sounds.

Cecilia followed, as did Bess, while the others held off in evident fear.

Although it was high noon, in the grove the heavy spruce and cedar trees darkened the place, and the farther the girls penetrated into the depths of the wood, the deeper did the shadows close in around them. Cora picked up a stout stick as she advanced.

"Get me one," begged Cecilia. "We may encounter a bear."

"Human?" asked Cora with a laugh.

"Preferably," answered Cecilia, keeping very close to Cora.

The noises had ceased. The girls halted, waiting for a sound to give them the clue of direction.

"He's dead!" gasped Cecilia. "It was the drink - he got the drink, and then died!"

"As long as he got it," whispered Cora. She was anxious to catch another "groan."

"There!" exclaimed Bess, as a sound, faint but decisive, was heard from a hollow ahead.

"Where?" asked Cora, purposely misunderstanding Bess.

"Here!" called Cecilia, who, with sudden resolve, had snatched the stick from Cora's hand, and now darted forward.

She went straight for the spring.

CHAPTER III

"NO BOYS!"

Such shouting and such laughing!

There, hidden in the thicket near the spring, were discovered Jack Kimball and Walter Pennington, while the chuckles and other noises emerging from mysterious parts of the wood indicated the presence of human beings, although the sounds had a queer similarity to that made by furry beasts.

"Oh, Clip! Spare me!" called Jack, as Cecilia actually undertook to punish physically the offending young man. "I really did not think you would be scared - in fact, I had an idea you were scare-immune "

"I am," declared the girl; "but the idea of me wasting sympathy! I might have discovered the dead man of all my life-long dreams - had to appear in court, and all the other delightful consequences of finding a man under suspicious circumstances; and there you are not even sick. Jack Kimball, how could you? You might at least have had the politeness to be deadly ill."

Walter crawled out from the thicket.

"I thought I smelled eating," he remarked, "and I suggested that we postpone the wild and woolly until we had investigated."

"Oh, come on," called Cora. "We may as well allow you to move on. - You have actually interrupted the plans for our first official run.'

"Good!" exclaimed Ed Foster, who, with some other young chaps, had collected themselves from the various haunts. "Any boys?"

"Boys!" echoed Cora.

"B-o-y-s!" drawled Maud, "chucking the imploring look," as Cecilia whispered to Cora.

"We have been discussing the question," declared Bess, as they all started toward the lunch spread on the grass, "and we have now fully decided. The answer is: No boys!"

This verdict brought forth the expected chorus of groans from the young men.

"Indeed, you may be glad to get a fellow when you find yourselves in a good and proper smashup," declared Jack, "and I predict a smash-up about every other mile."

The sight of the tempting lunch and that of the other young ladies who had not undertaken the march to the spring, was the signal for a "grand rush" - and that was about all.

When the boys extricated themselves from the "rush" there was not a crumb visible.

"We had all we wished," faltered the circumspect Ray Stuart. "You were entirely welcome - might have saved, at least, the dishes."

"Oh," breathed Ed, "it is so much pleasanter to poach - don't spoil it."

Ed cast a most appreciative glance at Ray. She expected it, of course, and accepted it with a smile.

Clip was talking earnestly to Jack, Cora was being entertained by Walter, who, at the same time, managed to keep up a running conversation with the group of girls now busy putting away the lunch things.

"We had a dreadful accident coming out," said Belle. "Bess ran over -"

"A square meal in a square basket," interrupted Bess. "I demolished the hamper that Ida Giles had bestowed on Sidney Wilcox. It was a peace offering, I believe."

"And you should have seen the kind of `pieces' Bess made of it," commented Hazel with a merry laugh.

"Hush!" hissed Ed with his finger to his lips.

"Something tells me that the demolished hamper forbodes evil. You will regret the day, Miss Elizabeth, that you spilled Sid Wilcox's -"

"Pumpkin pie," finished Cora. "I never saw such pumpkiny pumpkin pie in my life. I can smell it yet!"

"Mrs. Giles' famous home-made," quoted Walter. "Well, it might have been worse - they might have eaten that pie."

"Say, fellows," said Jack suddenly, "this is all very pretty - the girls, I mean, of course - but does it smite any one of you young rustics that we have an engagement - ahem! At three-thirty, wasn't it?"

"Precisely," declared Ed. "So much obliged for the feed; and do we make a party call?"

"Of course," answered the pretty Ray, attempting to tie her huge scarf, without having any idea of doing so. "We shall expect -"

"The bunch?" interrupted Jack, knowing Ray's preference for the handsome Ed.

"How -"

"Naughty," simpered Cecilia. "Jack, how can you use slang in the presence of ladies?" and she assumed the characteristic "tough" walk, which had always been one of Clip's most laughable capers.

"Loidies!" echoed Jack, tilting his cap and striking an attitude appropriate to that assumed by Cecilia. He slipped his arm within hers, and the pair "strutted off," in the fashion identified with the burlesque stage.

"Here! here!" called more than one young lady. "Come back here, Clip! There are to be no boys!"

"This isn't a boy," called back Cecilia, keeping up the performance. "He's only a -"

"Don't you dare!" threatened Jack.

The girls began to gather the things up from the grass.

"Now don't hurry," remarked Ed coolly. "The fact is, we are not going your way."

"Don't want us!" almost gasped Ray.

"Shook!" groaned Bess.

"Not at all," Walter hurried to add, "but the real truth is - well, let me see. What's the real truth?"

Jack was fetching Cecilia back. At some secret sign the young men actually took to their heels, and ran away before the girls realized what was happening. But from a distance they waved a cheerful adieu.

"What do you think of that!" exclaimed Hazel.

"Oh, they are just up to some frolic, and could not take us in," said Cora. "If we were not so busy with our plans we might follow them. But I propose continuing the business meeting."

With some reluctance, for the time had been greatly enlivened by the appearance of the young men on the scene, the girls once more got to discussing the details of their proposed three days' tour.

As Cora had predicted, Maud wanted the stops along the way made at the homes of her various and varied relatives. Daisy feared her mother would insist upon a chaperone, and this almost absorbed Daisy's chance of being eligible. Ray thought the motors should flaunt flags - pretty light blue affairs - but Bess declared it would be infinitely more important to carry plenty of gasoline.

So the girls planned and plotted, until, in the northwest, a great black cloud came stealing over the silent blue, gathering fury as it came, and coming very quickly at that.

"A storm!" shouted Belle. "Oh, I do hope it won't be the thundering kind!"

There was a swirl of the leaves around them, and the wind gave a warning howl. All ran for the cars.

"A tornado, likely," said Hazel. "And, oh, dear! this is just about the time that Paul will be bringing the mail over. I am so nervous since his firm undertook the mail route between New City and Cartown. This is such a lonely road for an auto in a storm - especially when every one knows Paul carries the mail."

Hazel was greatly agitated, but the other girls endeavored to reassure her.

"Why, Paul will be all right," declared Cora, surprised at Hazel's alarm. "What could happen to him? Why is a storm in the afternoon of such consequence?"

"Oh, I don't know," sighed Hazel; "but having to manage a car, and be personally responsible for the big mailbag - there is so much important mail between Cartown and New City - I have been nervous about it ever since Paul began carrying it."

"But it makes him all the more important to his firm," said Cora convincingly, "and I am sure he will be all right."

"You read too many wild-west stories," commented Bess, who was still alongside the Whirlwind with her Flyaway. "There are no stagecoach hold-ups these days."

"I hope not," returned Hazel with a forced laugh.

Quickly the storm was gathering. With some apprehension Cora directed the line of cars.

"You lead, Daisy," she said, "as your clothes are most perishable."

"Indeed," shouted Cecilia, "my `strained' nurse suit will have to go to the laundry if it gets wet, and that adds to the price - reduces my bargain."

"Well, hurry, at any rate," commanded Cora. "I know of a barn we may be able to make."

"We ought to meet Paul at the bridge," remarked Hazel, evidently unable to dismiss her concern for her brother.

"Now, Hazel," exclaimed Cora, her voice carrying something of vexation, "one would think you suspected -"

"You don't really think those boys would play a trick on him?" interrupted Hazel. "Somehow I didn't like the way they looked - as if they were plotting something."

Cora laughed heartily. "Why, you precious baby!" she managed to say; "do you think boys of their caliber would tamper with the mail? To say nothing of putting so nice a boy as Paul to inconvenience?"

"Oh, of course; forgive me, Cora. I should not have asked that. But you know what Paul and I are to each other!"

"Yes, I know," said Cora with marked emphasis. "You are each the other's little brother and sister. But it's nice, Hazel, very nice, and I forgive you the fling at Jack."

"And Ed?" asked Hazel mischievously.

"And Walter," added Cora, ignoring the personal.

"Oh, mercy!" yelled Belle. "We're going to have another fire and brimstone thunderstorm! Cora, make for that farmhouse!"

"Yes," called Cora, "I guess it will be all wind, and it won't hurt the machines. Turn for the cottage, girls!"

Blinding and brutal, the wind and sand attacked the eyes and ears of the motor girls, in spite of all the hoods and goggles. It was one of those tearing windstorms, that often come in summer, seemingly bent on raising everything on earth heavenward except the sand - that always sought refuge under eyelids - the average grain of sand would rather get in a girl's eye than help to make up a reputable mountain.

The line of cars made straight for the little farmhouse. It was sheltered in a clump of pines quite near the roadside.

Bess drew up first. Belle was out, and upon the steps of the porch. She had even struck the brass knocker before the others could bring their machines to a stop.

"Belle is frightened," said Ray, taking her time to leave Cecilia's auto.

"Well, we had a great storm one day - and Belle has the reflex action," explained Cora, referring to an exciting incident told of in the first book of this series.

The door of the cottage opened.

"Come on, girls!" called Belle. "We may come in - the lady says."

"Now - now for an adventure!" whispered Cecilia. "I can see it through the closed blinds! I see it under the knocker. I feel it in my gloves! Yes, young ladies, there is going to be something doing inside that cottage!"

CHAPTER IV

THE STRANGE PROMISE

When the eight young ladies marched into the little cottage it must be admitted that each had her misgivings. What would any one think of such a procession?

But Belle, whether from actual fright of the storm, or from some intuitive knowledge of the circumstances, seemed to be assured that they were all welcome.

A dark-eyed woman greeted them.

"Why, come right in," she insisted. "We haven't much room, but we are all glad to see you."

"Careful," whispered the mischievous Clip to Cora. "There's a trap door some place, I'll bet."

"Hush!" commanded Cora under her breath. "You will be suspected if not overheard."

The woman gathered up some sewing from an old-fashioned sofa. Cora saw instantly that the piece of furniture was of the most desirable pattern and quality, an antique mahogany gem of the colonial style.

"There will be room for most of us on your beautiful couch," said Cora, taking her place, and indicating that the others might follow. "What a handsome piece of furniture!"

"Yes," replied the woman with a sigh, "that is one of my family heirlooms. We are very fond of old furniture."

"Look out!" whispered the irrepressible Clip. "Perhaps the trap is in the sofa!"

Bess giggled helplessly.

Belle, with her self-confidence, peculiar to this particular occasion, took her place over by the window in a huge, straight-back chair - the kind built with "storm doors at the back."

The sad-eyed woman smiled with her lips, but her eyes "remained at half mast," as Clip put it.

"It is so delightful to meet a lot of healthy young ladies," began the woman, betraying a certain culture and unmistakable education. "I have a little daughter, who is not healthy of body, but her mind is the joy of our lives in this isolated place. She will ask to see you directly, and that is why I tell you of her infirmity. We never speak of it to her - she almost thinks herself in health. I am glad you came - for her sake."

Without waiting for a reply the woman opened a small door and disappeared:

"Now!" gasped Clip. "Now be prepared! We will be fed piece by piece, one by one, to the yellow dwarf -"

"Will you hush!" insisted Belle. "I am sure you ought to respect-"

"Oh, I do, Belle, dear! I respect your pretty self, and shall hate terribly to see you torn limb from -"

The opening of the door cut short Clip's nonsense.

The woman wheeled a child's invalid chair into the room. Sitting in this chair the girls beheld a child - that sort of child which heaven in making a cripple of seems to hold some special claim on. The lines of some amateur poet flashed across the mind of Cora:

"Does heaven in sending such as these,
From Nature hold a claim?
To keep them nearer to The Gates,
To call them in again?"

These lines had always appealed to Cora in spite of their faulty rhyme, and, in glancing at the little girl in the chair, she understood why.

"This is my daughter Wren," said the woman, "and I should have introduced myself. I am Mrs. Salvey Mrs. Ruth Salvey."

The girls gracefully acknowledged the introductions. Clip had surrendered - she was "all eyes on the little girl"; too absorbed to speak. She had left her place on the sofa, and now stood beside the invalid's chair.

"How do you do, Wren?" she managed to say finally, taking the small, white, slim hand within her own. "Aren't you frightened of - this invasion?"

"Oh, no, indeed," said the child sweetly. "I am perfectly delighted. Mother has been telling me all day we would have some pleasant surprise before night. I thought when I saw the storm coming that that was the surprise - I love storms, grandfather's kind - but now I know it is this."

Every girl in the room instantly felt the charm of this child. She was almost bewitching.

Her eyes had the same "unfathomable depths" that marked those of Mrs. Salvey, but the child did not otherwise resemble her mother. It was evident that the name Wren fitted her well

- so small, so sweet, so timid, and with such a whispering voice!

Then, her eyes were brown, her hair was brown and, in spite of ill-health, there was a gleam of color in her delicate cheeks.

"What's this?" asked Cora, stepping over to the child and touching a book in her lap.

"Oh, that - that is my story," replied Wren. "I want to tell you all about it. Will you have time to wait?" and she looked toward the window, through which could be seen the silent automobiles.

"Indeed, we will," replied Cora. "I am so anxious to hear all about it, and I am sure the others are. Do tell us, Wren," and Cora found a chair quite close to the one on wheels.

Cecilia was fairly "devouring the child." The others were plainly much interested. Belle, who evidently regarded the affair as her own particular "find," retained the slim hand of the invalid in that of her own healthy palm. Mrs. Salvey was smiling now - even the great sad eyes were throwing out a light, although the light did come from dark and uncertain depths.

Wren opened her book.

"This is my promise book," she began. "I have to tell you a long story about it. Then I will ask each of you to make me a promise - it is a very strange promise," she intoned most seriously. "But I know some day it will be kept. Some day all these promises will unite in one grand, great demand. Then Fate will have to answer."

CHAPTER V

A LITTLE BROWN WREN

The girls were awestricken.

Daisy, Maud, Hazel and Ray seemed to shrink closer together on the old mahogany sofa. Cora and the Robinson girls with Cecilia were grouped closely about the sick child.

"It's all about grandfather," she began. "I had the dearest, darlingest grandfather, and since he went away I am so lonely. Only for mother," she added, with something like an apology. "Of course, I am never really lonely with mother."

Mrs. Salvey shook her head. Then she picked up the discarded sewing.

"You see," went on Wren, "we used to live with grandfather in a beautiful cottage right near the river. He was a sea captain, and couldn't live away from the waves. Then I was strong enough to play on the sands."

Wren stopped. At the mention of her infirmity a cloud covered her young face. Presently she brightened up and resumed:

"But I am going to be strong again. When I find -"

She tossed her head back and seemed to see something beyond. For a moment no one spoke. The silence was, akin to reverence.

"Then," sighed the child, "when we lived by the ocean grandfather went out in a terrible storm - he said he had to go. And he never came back."

"Oh!" gasped Cora involuntarily.

Cecilia bent so close to Wren that her breath stirred the brown ringlets over the child's ears.

"But, of course," declared the child vehemently, "he will come back. If not here - in some other world."

"Dear," said Mrs. Salvey, "you had better make your story a little short. I am sure the young ladies will want to get over the roads before nightfall."

"Oh, it is quite early yet," declared Cecilia falsely, for the mantel clock pointed to six.

"I'll hurry," promised Wren. "You see, this is the important part of it all. When we lived with grandpa he made a beautiful table - I even helped him to make it. There were tiny pieces of wood all inlaid with anchors, oars and sea emblems. I used to dip them in the hot glue for grandpa. Well, there were some secret drawers in that table, and grandpa told me that if anything should happen to him we must explore the table. Well, we went away - it was the time of my own father's death - and when we came back the table was gone."

"Who took it?" demanded Cecilia sharply.

"Everything was sold - at auction - and no one could tell us anything about the table."

"You see," said Mrs. Salvey, "Wren thinks if we can find that table we will come into our own. Father was very fond of daughter, and the other relatives were so numerous that when the estate was equally divided it left very little for us. We thought the table might contain a will -"

"I know it did," declared Wren. "Didn't grandpa show it to me once? And now I want you each to sign the promise in my book. I shall read it over for you."

The child drew herself up straight, and held the book high between her hands. Then she read

"`I, the undersigned, promise most sacredly to do all in my power to help discover the whereabouts of an antique inlaid table that has on either side carved a large anchor, and which has the initials cut on each end, W. S. and R. S.'

These were mine and grandpa's initials," she explained. "I was called Wren because his name was Renton." She resumed reading the promise:

"`If ever I do discover this table I also promise to notify Wren Salvey immediately.' Then you sign," she said. "There are pen and ink. Mother always keeps them in the sitting-room for me."

Belle took the book. Pages were already filled with signatures.

"You must have a great many callers," she remarked, taking up the pen to sign.

"Oh, I take my book with me every time I go out," said Wren. "Sometimes mother takes me where there are a lot of people. I love to talk to folks."

"Of course you do," said Cora, filled with admiration for the mother who so humored the sick child. "And with all those promises, as you say, they must some day become a great, grand call, and so be answered."

"I hope you will hear the voice," said Wren fervently, and the day came when Cora remembered the child's prayer.

The girls added their names to the long list. Wren required that they repeat the promise individually, and, indeed, it became a most solemn proceeding.

The storm had entirely subsided. It was time to be on the road again, and Cora stood up first to take her leave.

"We really must go," she said. "We have had a most delightful hour. We shall never forget Wren, and, perhaps, some day we may return to fulfil our promise."

"I really feel that you will," declared the child. "I have never before met such - nice young ladies," and she blushed consciously. "I shall repeat your names many times - so that they will echo when I sleep."

Cecilia put her lips to the child's forehead. She did not dare trust herself to speak.

"I am sure you will dream about us - we are such an army," said Daisy with a laugh. "Try to forget that we are just girls -"

"She's an angel," interrupted Cecilia. "Don't get her mixed up with mere girls."

Wren laughed - such a dainty little laugh. She looked at Daisy.

"You are all - lovely," she declared, "and I always like blue eyes!"

Mrs. Salvey added her felicitations to those of her little daughter. "This has indeed been a most enjoyable visit," she said, "and I hope you will all try to keep your strange promise. I believe where one is so serious as is Wren something good is sure to result. If we could find that table -"

"Perhaps you will," said Cora pleasantly. "We are about to start on a long trip. We will make numbers of stops, and I assure you we will never forget to look for the table. I am sure it will give us a very pleasant duty to keep our eyes open."

"Indeed, it will," declared Cecilia warmly. "I only hope I shall be the lucky one - for I feel a sort of premonition that some one in this party really will be the means of bringing little Wren the good news. I have a mental picture of the table. I shall know it instantly."

"It would be very easy to recognize it," said Mrs. Salvey, opening the door as her visitors filed out. "The inlaid anchors are most conspicuous on the leaves."

Outside Cecilia renewed her antics. "Stick a hatpin in me - somebody do!" she exclaimed. "But not yours, Ray. I never could stand for that college, even in a stick."

Ray smiled and hurried into her car. The fair chauffeurs cranked up quickly, for it was almost dusk, and there was considerable road to cover between the place and Chelton.

"We must make speed now," called Bess. "I have a dinner date, be it known."

"I'm in a hurry, too," shouted Maud. "I have an engagement to be tried on - my new auto cloak. I have to have that on time."

The machines were speeding along merrily. It was pleasant after the rain, and the twilight lent enchantment to the delights of motoring.

"Why do you suppose Hazel was so anxious about Paul?" Bess asked Belle. "She could talk of nothing else, even when we were at the cottage."

"Well," replied the prudent Belle, "Hazel knows. There must

be some danger or she would not talk of it. Perhaps Paul has had some warning."

CHAPTER VI

THE HOLD-UP

Dashing over the country roads, the motor girls sent their machines ahead at fast speed, unwilling to stop to light up, and anxious to make the town before the twilight faded into nightfall.

Suddenly Cora, who was in the lead, grabbed the emergency brake and quickly shut off the power.

"What's that?" she asked. "Something straight ahead. Don't you see it, Hazel?"

Hazel stood up and peered into the gathering darkness.

"Yes; it looks like an auto. Perhaps some one got disabled, and had to leave the machine," she replied.

"Perhaps," returned Cora, going along carefully.

"It is an auto," declared Hazel presently, as they were almost upon the object in the roadway.

"The auto stage!" exclaimed Cora. "Don't be frightened, Hazel," she hurried to say. "Paul is not in it. He must have gone on with the mail."

Hazel sank down in the cushions and covered her eyes.

Somehow she could not bear to look at the deserted auto stage.

The other girls were coming along cautiously - they saw that something was the matter.

The standing machine was directly in the road; it instantly struck Cora that this was strange. Who could have been so careless as to leave an unlighted auto in the roadway, and night coming on?

She turned her wheel to guide the Whirlwind to one side, and then stopped. Bess was next, and she shut off the power from the Flyaway.

"What is it?" asked Bess anxiously. Belle did not venture to leave the machine, but Hazel had bounded out of the Whirlwind almost before Cora had time to stop it.

"Oh," exclaimed Hazel, "there are Paul's gloves. Where can he be?"

"Perhaps playing a trick on us," suggested Cora, although she had little faith in the possibility. "I am sure he would not go far off and leave this expensive machine here."

By this time all the other girls had reached the spot, and were now deliberating upon the abandoned auto. Suddenly a call - shrill and distinct - startled them.

"That's Paul!" shrieked Hazel, turning instantly and dashing off in the direction from which the voice had come. Cora, Bess, Maud and Cecilia followed her. Over the wet fields, through briars and underbrush the girls ran, while the call was repeated; this time there being no possibility of mistake - it was Paul shouting.

Breathless, the girls hurried on. With a sister's instinct Hazel never stumbled, but seemed to get over every obstacle like some wood sprite called to duty.

"Oh, I'm all right, girls! Take your time!" came the voice in the woods.

"All right!" repeated Hazel in uncertain tones.

"Oh, look!" shrieked Cecilia. "Didn't I tell you it was a joke? Look!"

What a sight! There, sitting on something like a stool, with a big cotton umbrella opened over his head, his eyes blinded with something dark, and his hands and feet made secure, was Paul Hastings, the chauffeur of the auto stage.

"Whatever does this means?" asked Cora, hurrying to Hazel, who was now madly snatching the black silk handkerchief from her brother's eyes.

"A prisoner of war," replied Paul rather unsteadily. "Glad you came, girls - there, sis, in my back pocket, you will find a knife. Just cut those carpet rags off my feet and hands."

Cecilia found the pocket knife, and, more quickly than any boy might have done it, she severed the bonds, and Paul stretched out - free.

"Well," he exclaimed, "this is about the limit!"

"Did the boys do it?" asked Cora.

"Boys! Not a bit of it," replied Paul. "It was a regular hold-up. And the mail! I must get that, if they have left it on the road. Did you see the car? Is it all right?"

"It appeared to be," said Cora. "It was the car that brought us to a standstill. It's in the middle of the road."

Paul shook himself as if expecting to find some damage to limb or muscle. Then he turned toward the open path.

"Tell us about it," demanded Cecilia. "Wasn't it a joke?"

"Joke!" he reiterated. "Well, I should say not! Would you call it a joke to have two masked men jump in front of a running car, and flash something shiny? Then to have them climb in, cover my eyes and tell me I would be all right, and not to worry!"

"Oh," sighed Hazel, "I felt something would happen to you, Paul, dear. You must give up this position."

"Well, we will see about that," he replied. "Perhaps I won't have anything to say about it - if the mailpouch is gone."

"Then they brought you out here?" asked Cecilia, determined to hear all the story.

"Carried me like a baby," replied Paul, "and in sheer humane consideration they put me near the road, so that my call might be heard."

"And the umbrella?" asked Cora.

"Oh, they went to a barn for that. It was raining, and my polite friends did not want me to take cold."

His tone was bitterly cutting; taking cold would evidently have been of small account to him.

"And they sat you upon that log?" put in Maud.

"Like any ordinary bump," he rejoined. "I never knew the misery of a bump on a log before."

"And, you are not hurt?" Hazel pressed close to his side and looked up lovingly at the tall boy.

"Not in the least - that is, physically. But I am seriously hurt mentally."

Cora could not but recognize how handsome Paul was. The excitement seemed to fire his whole being, and throw some subtle human phosphorus - a light from his burning brain certainly brightened in his eyes and even in his cheeks.

"Come along, girls," he said hurriedly. "Never mind the paraphernalia. Some lonely goat might like the rags. Let's get out on the road."

His anxiety was of course for the mail. That leather bag meant more to him than the mere transference of Uncle Sam's freight - it meant his honor - his position.

Over the rough fields the girls followed him. Hazel clung to his hand like a little sister indeed, while the others were content to keep as close as the uncertain footing would allow.

Presently they reached the road, then the stage coach. The other girls, who had not run to Paul's rescue, were standing around breathless.

Paul jumped into the car - thrust his hand into the box under the floor, where he always put the government pouch.

He brought up the mailbag.

CHAPTER VII

A CHANCE MEETING

Paul lost no time in reaching Cartown with the belated mail, and so was obliged to leave the girls an the road with scant ceremony, hardly pausing to discuss why he had been bound when no apparent robbery had been perpetrated.

Hazel appeared so agitated that Cora insisted upon her returning to the Kimball home to dinner, and also had succeeded in getting a promise from Paul that he would come there as early in the evening as it would be possible for him to do so.

Then, when the mail car was lost sight of, and the motor girls started again on their homeward way, Clip insisted upon leading.

"I know the variety of bandit," she declared, "and I want to meet him personally. He is sure to fall dead in love with me on the spot. And, oh, girls! Think of it! Me and the bandit!"

Even Hazel laughed. The suggestion called up a picture of the disgraceful Clip in robber uniform, with the proverbial red handkerchief on her head, and all the rest of the disreputable accessories. Clip would "look the part."

But the Thayer machine was not noted for its beauty or service - it had the reputation of bolting always at the "psychological moment," and when Clip dashed forward to meet her fate, the fate of the Turtle (as her car was called) intercepted her.

With a jerk the Turtle tossed up its head, bounced Clip off her seat, and then stopped.

"Oh!" exclaimed the girl. "Isn't this the utmost! And I about to meet my bandit! Now I suppose I will have to leave Turtle here to afford the foe a means of escape. I say, girls, isn't that the utmost?"

She jumped out of the car and, with a superficial glance at the fractious machine, waited for Cora's car.

"Come on, Ray," she said to her companion. "No use sitting there. That car will never, move unless it is dragged. I know her. No use monkeying with tools. When she stops, she stops, and we may as well make up our minds to it."

"But," argued Ray, "you have not even attempted to find out what is the matter. Perhaps we could fix it up -"

"No use attempting. I would find the whole thing the matter. Just feel," she suggested, putting her ungloved hand on the radiator. "You could make beef stew on any of her lids. Oh, I know this kind of hot box! I've boiled the water, and the cylinders are stuck."

By this time the other girls had come along. Cora insisted upon looking over the disabled machine, and, while she did so, Clip deliberately made herself comfortable in the Whirlwind.

"Get in with Daisy," she called to Ray. "This will do me."

"Can't we tow it?" asked Cora. "Why should you leave your machine out here? And it is almost dark!"

"That's the reason," replied Clip. "It is almost dark, and I prefer to leave the machine here as a little token of my love to the bandit. Suppose I want to be `run in' for traveling without a glimmer'?"

Cora saw that argument was useless. Reluctantly she turned from the Turtle. Ray climbed in with Daisy and Maud. Bess and Belle were ready to start "from the seat," without cranking up. Cora gave the Whirlwind a few turns.

"I hope we get home without any further trouble," came from the folds of Ray's blue veil. "I think we have had enough for one day."

"Enough!" echoed Clip. "Why, I could stand ten times that much! I love trouble - in the abstract."

"Suppose you call this the abstract," almost sneered Daisy, who evidently did not relish being crowded.

"Certainly I do," declared Clip. "Just gaze on the abstracted Turtle!"

"Who's that?" whispered Hazel nervously. A step could be heard in the roadway.

"My bandit!" breathed Clip. "Oh, my darling, desperate bandit!"

"Hush!" cautioned Cora, for she felt the possibility of Paul's captors being about still. Then two figures appeared from the sharp turn in the road. Cora wanted to start, but hesitated. The figures came closer. They were those of two well-dressed men; that was easily discernable.

Clip put her hand over her heart.

"Oh-h=h!" she groaned audibly. "Isn't he handsome!"

Hazel clutched at her sleeve. "Do stop!" she begged. "They may be -"

"They are!" answered Clip, and, as the, men halted beside the Turtle, she deliberately jumped out and approached them.

The other girls were spellbound. Cora, too, left her place - she knew Cecilia's recklessness and felt it her duty to stand by her.

The two strange men looked first at the girls and then at the car.

"Had an accident?" asked the taller of the two politely.

"Oh, no, it's chronic," answered Clip flippantly, much to Cora's dismay.

The men were evidently gentlemen. They were well dressed, and had the mannerisms of culture.

"Perhaps I can help you," suggested one, taking from his pocket a wrench. "I always carry tools - meet so many `chronics,' " and he laughed lightly.

"Come on," called Hazel from the Whirlwind. "You know, Paul will be waiting, Cora."

At this the men both started. He with the wrench ceased his attempt to open the motor hood. The other looked toward Hazel.

"Oh, I see," he said with affected ease. "Your friend promised to meet you, and you are late."

"My brother," said Hazel curtly.

"Paul Hastings," said Cora quickly, before she knew why.

"Oh!" almost whistled the taller man. "I see; of the Whitehall Company?"

"Do you know him?" demanded Cora rather sharply.

"Slight-ly," drawled the stout man, he with the wrench.

"Well, we had best not detain you, young ladies," said the other, "as you have so important an engagement," and with that they both turned off.

"What do you think of that?" exclaimed Cora.

"The utmost!" replied Clip, in her favorite way of expressing "the limit."

"They knew Paul!" gasped Hazel.

"Seemed to," answered Cora evasively. She had her opinions and doubts as to who these gentlemen might be.

"Just my luck," murmured Clip. "I rather liked the tall fellow, but I noticed that the other carried a gold filigree fountain pen, had a perfectly dear watch charm, and he talked like a lawyer."

"Oh, my!" exclaimed Cora. "You did size him up. I only noticed that he was a joint short on his right-hand thumb."

"That, my dear, is termed a professional thumb-mark. We will know him if we meet him in the dark," said Clip.

Cora laughed. She felt, however, more serious than she cared to have the others know. "Well, let's be off this time," she said. "We will hardly make town before dark now."

CHAPTER VIII

JACK AND CLIP

"A deliberate trick of Cecilia's," murmured Daisy.

"She pretends to be so off-hand," answered Maud. "I have always noticed that that sort of girl is the greatest schemer."

"To leave her car out on the road, and then boldly ask Jack Kimball to go with her to fetch it. Who ever heard of such a thing? I wonder Cora tolerates her."

"Cora is what some people call `easy,' " said Daisy with uncertain meaning. "She takes her chances in choosing friends."

"Did they fetch the car back?"

"I saw it at the garage this morning. I do hope it cannot be fixed. I mean," Maud hurried to say, "I hope she will not hamper us with it on our tour. It is only fit for the junkman."

Daisy and Maud were walking toward the post office. It was the morning after the adventure on the road, and the two girls had heard from Ray Stuart something of the news they were now discussing. The hold-up of Paul Hastings was to them not so important as the fact that Cecilia Thayer had gone over to Kimball's and actually asked Jack Kimball to take her out Woodbine way to tow home the balky Turtle.

But, precisely as her friend had said, Clip was a schemer. In the first place, she had no idea of detaining her companions on the lonely road to "monkey with the machine," so soon after Paul's hold-up. Next, she had no idea of leaving the car there at the mercy of fate. Instead, she deliberately went over to Kimball's after dinner, asked Jack to take her out Woodbine way, and incidentally suggested that he take along a gun. Jack had two good friends, each opposite the other in type. Bess Robinson was very much admired by him; and Cecilia Thayer, she who always played the tomboy to the extent of affording a good time for others when she could actually disguise a serious reason in the joke, she who affected the "strained" nurse costume for fun, when it was a real necessity - Jack Kimball liked Cecilia Thayer. Her rather limited means often forced her to make sport of circumstances, but, in every case, Cecilia "won out." She was, the boys said, "no knocker."

So it happened as Daisy related. Clip did ask Jack to go with her to fetch home the car. It also happened that they encountered Sid Wilcox on the way. He seemed to be returning alone in his auto from Cartown. Sid told Ida, Ida told Ray, Ray told Daisy and Daisy told Maud.

Daisy and Maud were inseparable chums. They agreed on everything - from admiration for Jack Kimball and Walter Pennington, to dislike for Cecilia Thayer, and something akin to jealousy for the Robinson girls. Cora was beyond criticism - they simply "regarded her."

"And," spoke Daisy, as they turned into the green, "I do believe that the boys played that trick on Paul. I thought when they hurried so to get away that they were up to something."

"Queer joke," commented Maud.

"Didn't you think those strange men acted suspiciously?" asked Daisy.

"How could they do otherwise when Cecilia acted as she did? I never saw a girl so forward."

"I suppose she will have some boys tagging after us on our tour, if her car is fixable," went on Daisy in sarcastic tones. "Likely she will find some excuse for stopping at hotels, and such places. Mother insisted I should not go to any public eating place unless we have some older person along. But Cecilia - she is old or young, just as it suits her."

"There's Bess and Belle!" exclaimed Maud, as the Robinson twins' runabout swerved into the avenue.

"And there are Jack - and Cecilia!" Daisy fairly gasped the words.

At that instant the two last named persons, in Jack's little car, came up to the turn. Cecilia looked almost pretty - even her critics admitted that, secretly. Of course, Jack was always handsome.

"I wonder how Bess feels," remarked Daisy with scornfully curled lip.

"She thinks a lot of Jack," replied Maud, as both bowed to the occupants of the runabout.

"Where do you suppose they are going?" went on Daisy.

"Oh, probably to see about having the old car fixed up. Of course, when she got Jack to fetch it she will manage to have him attend to the rest."

Bess and Belle were now abreast of the girls on the sidewalk. The twins bowed pleasantly, while the others nodded in return.

"I wish mother had not gone to town this morning," said Daisy. "I would just like to see where they are all going."

"Your mother took the car?"

"Yes; and she won't be home until evening. Well, I declare if there isn't Cora and -"

"Walter Pennington," finished Maud. "She is almost as changeable as her brother."

"Isn't it too mean that we have to walk," complained Daisy. "I have a mind to go over to the garage and ask for a car. Father often gets one."

"Oh, yes. Doctors are always having breakdowns. Do you suppose you could get one?"

"Well, I am going to try, at any rate," and Daisy Bennet quickened her pace, while Maud Morris hurried along with her companion. It was but a few minutes' walk to the garage, and when the girls reached the entrance they were surprised to find the three automobiles, Jack's, Cora's and the twins' pulled up outside.

"Oh, I can't go in now," demurred Daisy. "We will have to wait until they go. Funny they should be taking a morning run, without asking us along."

Paul Hastings was talking to the Robinson girls. It was evident that he was much excited. Cora was on the sidewalk, and Cecilia was beside her. Jack stood off to one side with Walter.

"Some important consultation," whispered Daisy. "I'll wager it's about the hold-up."

"Of course, father knows you had nothing to do with it," Bess was saying to Paul, "but he is positive the papers were in that mail. Corn, thought it best we should let you know right away."

"Forewarned is forearmed," said Paul. Then Daisy and Maud

came up to the group.

"My!" exclaimed Daisy. "Quite a gathering."

"Yes," answered Clip. "We are glad you came. Now our meeting is complete. We want evidence. Tell us all you know about the strange men. You had a good chance to observe. You were not in the little quadrille on the road."

"Why," stammered Daisy, "I thought them very nice-looking men. They were well dressed, and -"

"That's it," interrupted Jack. "They were nice men, well dressed. What else do you expect young ladies to observe? Clip, your suspicions are not borne out by facts. Not a girl in the party but yourself saw - what was it? The corner of the missing blue envelope in the upper right-hand pocket -"

"Jack Kimball! You know perfectly well I never said such a thing. I did see something blue, but it might have been -"

"A captured shadow from Daisy's eyes," said Walter dryly.

"What happened?" breathed Maud. Then Walter realized what a girl's eyes may do in the matter of "imploring." He deliberately stepped over to Maud's side.

"Oh, some valuable papers were taken from the mailbag," volunteered Clip. "And we thought the strange men might have found them."

"You cheerful fibber," whispered Jack. "Come on, if you expect to get to Cartown to-day."

"How can we, now?" asked Clip in an undertone.

"Just jump in and go," replied Jack. "Why should we explain?"

Jack cranked up his car, and in her usual deliberate way,

Cecilia Thayer stepped into the runabout, pulled on her gloves, smoothed out the robe, and then said: "Good morning!"

Jack and Clip left the others standing in surprise and, perhaps, disappointment. Only Cora guessed where they were actually going.

CHAPTER IX

THE MYSTERIOUS RIDE

The fact that Cecilia Thayer could be old or young, as had been remarked by one of her companions, was not a mere saying. The Thayers were strangers in Chelton, and Cecilia was now only home from school on a vacation. It was generally understood that the girl was not exactly a daughter of the small household, but perhaps a niece, or some relative, who made her home with the people. She never invited her friends to her home, but this was not considered strange, as her means plainly were not equal to the circumstances of those with whom she associated.

Not that Cecilia sought this class, because she was constantly sought by them - she was a brilliant, happy young girl, and, as such, was a most desirable adjunct to the Chelton younger set.

It was, of course, Cora Kimball who "took her up," and that fact was sufficient to vouch for all

The girl and Jack were well on the road to Woodbine the morning of the little meeting by the garage, when, with a very different expression of countenance to that shown to the party by the roadside, Cecilia grasped at the arm of the young man beside her.

"It's awfully good of you, Jack," she said, "and I suppose I am taking desperate chances."

"Good! The idea! It's a privilege," he answered warmly.

"You suspect, of course."

"I have suspected," he said with a light laugh.

"And if the girls find out?"

"What of it? Is it a disgrace to -"

"Hush! I haven't qualified yet, and when I do I'm going to spring it on them." She tossed her head back defiantly. "Won't some of them howl!"

Jack laughed outright. "You're a brick, Clip," he exclaimed. "You can count on Cora, too. Does she know?"

"I haven't told her, but I imagine she has guessed. You are a great family at guessing."

"Which way?" he inquired, nodding toward a fork in the road.

"To the left. Isn't it too mean that our old lumber wagon gave way? I never had more need of it. It's just splendid of you to help me out this way."

"And good of you to let me," he replied with a keen glance at the girl's bright face.

"Of course I had no idea of going on the girls' trip. I only went in for the arrangements for the fun of the thing. I seem to need an awful lot of fun," she finished with a sigh that ended like a groan.

"Oh, we all do, more or less," spoke Jack. "Only some of us are more upright than others in the way we acknowledge it."

They were turning up to the Salvey cottage. Cecilia pointed it out.

"You must expect to sign the promise book," she said. "That is a condition of admittance."

"So Cora told me. Well, I'll sign. Can't tell which name may win the prize."

"Of course I'll see Wren first. But before we go she will insist upon seeing you. And - don't mind her extravagances about me. You know, she sees so few people that she thinks I am just wonderful."

"I agree with her. But you can count upon my discretion, if that is what you want, Clip."

"You're `immense,' Jack!" exclaimed the girl, her smile apologizing for the vulgarity of the expression. "If I had a brother like you -"

"Hush! Your brother! Why, Clip "

"Here we are," she interrupted; and she prepared to get out as Jack stopped the car. "Suppose you stay outside until I call you?"

"Oh, if I must. But be sure to call. I've had Cora play that trick, and forget the cue."

"Oh, she'll have to see you," and with that Cecilia jumped out of the car, and presently touched the brass knocker of the little cottage.

Jack was left to his own thoughts. Wasn't she a girl, though? So like Cora in her impulses. Well, a girl has to be impulsive to get ahead - she is so ridiculously hampered by conventionalities.

It seemed a long time before Clip reappeared at the door, and beckoned him to come in. Then the room he entered smelled strongly of antiseptics, and the crippled child sat in a chair made sweet and fresh with snowy pillows. Wren had her promise book in her hands. Briefly Cecilia introduced Jack, while the child eyed him keenly, as do those deprived of the usual means of making sure of their friends.

"You know about my promise," she said shyly. "Grandpa's will is lost in an old table, and will you promise to help find it?"

"Indeed I will," said Jack warmly, taking the pen offered. "I have a weakness for hunting old furniture, and I hope it will be my good fortune to find the table."

"How much you are like your sister," said Wren, referring to Cora, "but not a bit like your cousin."

This caused both Jack and Cecilia to laugh - she Jack's cousin!

Mrs. Salvey patted the child's head. "She is so much better lately," she said, "since she has been friends with Miss Thayer."

"Her friendship is wonderful," said Jack, handing back the book. "It does me all sorts of good."

Cecilia was pulling on her gloves. She picked up the small black satchel (her hand bag, she called it), and started for the door.

"That hand bag smells like -"

"Fresh eggs," she interrupted Jack. "Understand, young man, I had to come out here to get one dozen of strictly fresh eggs."

For a moment she looked intently at Jack, as if determined to put him on his honor without further explanation. He took her hand and assisted her into the car. As he did so she felt the assurance that Jack Kimball was her friend.

Then they started back to Chelton.

CHAPTER X

"THEY'RE OFF!"

"Isn't it too mean? I never thought that Cecilia would act so. I think Jack knows why."

Bess Robinson was talking to Cora. Her voice betrayed something other than disappointment. Bess now called Cecilia by her full name - the affectionate "Clip" had been laid aside. Besides this she hesitated when Jack's name was needed in her conversation. The fact was perfectly evident. Jack's attention to Cecilia, their runaway ride, and the consequent talk, had rather hurt Bess. Jack had always been a very good friend to her.

"But Clip simply can't come," said Cora. "Her machine is out of order, and, besides this, she is called away to look after some sick relative."

"Cora Kimball!" exclaimed Bess. "You're a perfect baby. Sick relative! Why, every one sickens a relative when they want to go away in a hurry. It might be interesting to know who else has a made-up sick relative who demands, say, Jack's immediate attention."

"Why, Bess! I'm surprised that you should speak so bitterly. You know perfectly well that Jack's going to the races. You heard them make all the arrangements - Jack, Ed and Walter. Besides -"

Cora stopped. She tossed back her pretty head as if too disgusted to speak. She was packing the last of her touring things into the hampers of the Whirlwind. She would have everything ready for the early start next morning. Bess Robinson had run over for final instructions, when Cora announced that Cecilia Thayer could not go with them on the motor girls' tour. This information drove all other details from the mind of Bess. And now Cora was locking her boxes.

"Oh, I suppose we will get along very well without her," said Bess finally. "In fact, it may be better that she does not come, for she is bound to be doing things that are risky."

"Well, we will miss her, I'm sure," said Cora, "for she is such good company. But we will have to manage."

"Has Belle all your tools packed? Don't forget candles; they are so handy when anything happens after dark. I always fetch them. They poke under little places so nicely."

"Oh, I fancy Belle has managed to take along the candelabra. At least, I think I can count on the glass candlesticks. Poor Belle! I wonder will she ever leave off that sort of thing. She cares more or an `effect' than for a good square meal," answered Bess.

"Alt kinds make a world," replied Cora. "Suppose she were as sensible as you or I? Why, as well take away the flowers, and plant kindling wood.

Bess laughed. Cora turned up the path with her. "I met Ray," said Bess, "buying a new veil, of course. I would hate to be as pretty as Ray, and have so much trouble to keep up the reputation. That's the worst of pretty girls. They really have to keep pretty."

"And Daisy? Was she buying a new novel to read en route? They might both do better to `chip in' and buy a new kit of tools," said Cora.

At precisely eight forty-five o'clock the next morning the Whirlwind drew up in front of the post-office. The start was to be made from that point, and Cora was first to arrive. With her were Hazel Hastings, and Gertrude Adams, a school friend of Cora's.

Two minutes later the Flyaway puffed into sight with the Robinson twins smiling serenely from her two-part seat.

Scarcely had the occupants of the two car exchanged greetings than Daisy Bennet and Maud Morris drove up in the Bennet runabout, called the Breeze. On account of the change of plan, Ray Stuart was to ride with Cora, instead of with Clip, as was at first proposed. Ray met the girls at the post-office. As predicted, she did look like a brand new bisque statue. She wore a soft silk coat, of light green pongee, the same shade hood, over which "rested," one might say, a long white chiffon veil. It reposed on the hood, where two secret pins held it, but otherwise the veil was mingled with Ray's expression and the surrounding atmosphere. The girls sighed as they beheld her. She had been waiting for some minutes in the post-office, and needless to say there were others waiting, too - not altogether engrossed in reading the latest mail.

Cora stepped out of the Whirlwind and opened the tonneau door for Ray. Hazel and she were to ride within the car, while Gertrude shared the seat with Cora. Cora wore her regular motor togs. The close-fitting pongee coat showed off well her perfect figure, and with the French bonnet, that nestled so snugly to her black tresses there was no semblance to the flaring, loose effect so common to motorists. She looked more like a Paris model than a girl equipped for a tour. But Cora had that way - she was always "classy," as the boys expressed it, or in perfect style, as the girls would admit.

Hazel usually affected strong shades - she was dark and could wear reds and browns to good advantage. It so happened that the motor girls afforded a peculiar variety, no two wearing similar outfits. Timid little Maud Morris was in white, and

Daisy was in linen. The Robinson girls wore their regular uniform - Bess in Havana-brown and Belle in true-blue. So it will be seen that such an array of beauty and clothes could not help but attract attention, to say nothing of the several automobiles that made up the procession in front of the post-office.

At the last moment Belle had to run into a store to make some trifling purchases, while Daisy sent two extra postcards, and Ray needed something from the drug store.

Finally all was ready. It was just nine o'clock.

"Ready!" called Cora.

A blast on a bugle startled them. Then -

What was it?

It looked like a hay wagon, but it came along at the speed of a fine auto.

"The boys!" called the girls in one breath.

Sure enough, there were Jack, Walter, Ed and some others of their chums, piled up on a veritable hay rack, and they wore all sorts of farmer clothes. The hay rack evidently set upon the body of are automobile.

And Jack on the "monkey seat," blowing that bugle!

"Start!" called Cora.

"They're off!" shouted the chorus from the hay wagon, and then Chelton folks were treated to a sight the like of which they had never before witnessed.

It was the first official tour of the original motor girls.

CHAPTER XI

THOSE DREADFUL BOYS

"No BOYS, eh?" shouted Ed from his "perch" in the hay.

"Aren't they dreadful?" exclaimed Daisy with doubtful sincerity.

"Hope mother doesn't hear of it," replied Maud. "She would be sure to worry."

Cora laughed, and Bess fairly panted. Belle tossed something into the hay wagon as it passed - it made a practice of passing each machine in turn, and then doing it all over again.

Every one in Chelton and the near-by places rushed out as the procession went along. It was like a circus - many folks really did believe that a "railroad show" had come to town unannounced.

The girls had planned to have dinner at a pretty little tea-house on the outskirts of Hollyville. But the boys had no intention of turning back, it seemed, and imagine those boys in the tea-house, kept by a couple of enterprising college girls!

"Hey there!" called Jack. "When do we eat? There's the noon whistles."

"Yon don't eat," replied Cora.

"Don't, eh? Well, look out for your commissary department," answered Jack. "We came prepared to fight."

"Oh," sighed Daisy, "do you suppose they will spoil all our boxes?"

"I'm sure I don't know," replied the noncommital Maud.

But Hazel said: "What do you suppose they are up to?"

"Trust them for fun," answered Cora. "I will simply trounce Jack if he attempts to overhaul our stores."

Hazel laughed merrily. "If only Paul were along," she ventured. "And, Cora, do you know that mailbag business is not by any means settled?" she asked.

"I know that, girlie," said Cora with polite seriousness, "but all troubles are tabooed on this ride, you know. Gertrude," to the girl who had been looking and listening, "I appoint you monitor of this car. The first girl to bring in troubles is to be fined."

"Very well," replied Gertrude, "I shall be glad to have something to do. I feel like a stranger with those boys."

"That's because you do not know them," ventured Ray. "They are perfectly splendid boys."

"Make a note of that," called Cora. "Gertrude, that is one mark in favor of Ray."

The procession was winding along a pretty country road. Trees closed in from side to side, and deep gutters outlined the driveway from the footpath.

The boys had actually ceased their antics for the time, and it occurred to more than one girl that this respite might have been more advantageous if it had been put into operation in the city streets - the decorum was wasted in the woods. But boys have a queer reasoning code - where girls are concerned.

"Don't you suppose they will turn back before we reach the Glen?" called Bess to Cora. Their machines were running quite close together.

"If they don't leave us we will drive past the teahouse, and come back later," said Cora.

"But what will the college girls think? They will be sure to have a nice lunch ready."

"When Tillie sees Ed Foster she will cease to think. She knows Ed," and Cora laughed significantly.

"Oh, look!" shouted Hazel. "A flock of sheep. And directly in the track. The boys -"

At that moment every one saw the sheep. The hay wagon made a spurt and dashed straight through the frightened herd, scattering them right and left, like feathers blown by the wind.

Daisy and Maud came next. They had time to jam down the brakes, but it would have been wiser to have dashed through the flock without loss of time, for an angry ram turned as the car slacked speed, and when Daisy and Maud saw him jump toward them, they also jumped out into the gutter, deserting their car.

A big, woolly ram leaped up from the midst of the flock, and actually landed in the runaway automobile. The improvised hay wagon was quickly steered to one side, just as Daisy's car, with the horned beast at the wheel, plunged past.

The machine, in charge of the queer mechanician, plunged straight ahead, and after a moment's hesitation on the part of their drivers, the other cars were quickly sent after it.

The boys shouted lustily. As if the frightened and angry ram cared for the harmony of a college quartet. Wasn't it ridiculous to see the ram positively driving the car?

By some strange instinct the animal had raised its fore legs to the rim of the steering wheel, standing upright on his hind ones, which were jamming the brake and clutch pedals.

"Oh l" screamed the girls in a chorus. "There comes a runabout! He'll collide with it!"

A runabout, coming in the opposite direction, and headed straight for the ram, could be seen down the road. The driver was a girl, that was evident, but she was so muffled in hood, veil and cloak that her features were not discernible.

"Stop it!" screamed Gertrude. "She'll be killed."

The ram evidently saw the other car coming, and tried to leap out, but its fore feet had gone through the spaces between the spokes of the steering wheel. The girl in the runabout was sending her car from side to side, in a frantic endeavor to avoid a collision. It seemed to be a choice with her, whether she should smash into the ram's car, or tilt into the roadside ditch.

Suddenly the girl stood up. The eyes of the motor girls and their boy companions were on her. She gave a scream, and then - something happened. From the rear cars came a scream. Then - the Breeze was stopped - the ram was gone, and the runabout was ditched.

Where and who was the unfortunate driver?

CHAPTER XII

THE GIRL IN THE DITCH

When all the machines had been stopped there was a wild rush to the rescue - Bess and Belle with Gertrude hurrying back to where Daisy and Maud had been left, while Cora, Ray and Hazel ran forward to the side of the strange runabout. The boys divided themselves - some going in each direction.

Presently Cora shouted

"Jack! Jack! Hurry! It's Clip! And she is unconscious!"

Jack was not far away, and at his sister's call he hurried to her. Ray had taken Cecilia's head in her lap, while Cora was trying to lift the unconscious girl from her bent-up posture in the narrow, roadside, grass-grown ditch.

"Oh, the poor dear!" sighed Cora. "To think that our sport should have -"

Cecilia was opening her eyes.

"Clip! Clip, dear!" whispered Cora. "Try to - wake up!"

Cecilia did try - she put her hand to her dazed eyes.

"Here! Let me lift her," commanded Jack, slipping down on the other side into the deep grass and without any apparent effort lifting Cecilia up. With one long step he reached the road. Then for a moment he seemed uncertain - should he lay the girl down, or carry her to a machine?

"Oh, I can stand," she said faintly. "I am much better now. What - happened?"

"You happened," answered Jack, so dismissing the question. "Just keep still, and we will have you around directly. This is where you beat the motor girls." He was now helping her to her feet. "You may ride back with the motor boys."

"Are you better?" asked Ray anxiously, stroking Cecilia's white hand, which had been divested of its glove. "Wasn't it dreadful?"

"Very," sighed Cecilia. "And my poor little machine! Jack, how can I ever -"

"You can never," he insisted with a wink. "I never saw such a rambunctious ram. Didn't he ramify, though?"

"What in the world was it?" asked Cecilia. She was sitting on the grass and seemed almost prepared to laugh. "I thought I must be seeing things. Then I -"

"Felt things," said Jack. "That's the regular course of the disease. Here come the others. Hello, Daisy has the veil tied up, and Maud is limping."

"What happened to them?" asked Cecilia.

"Same thing that happened to you," replied Jack. "The ram. That was the most happening thing I have seen in some time."

Maud was limping, and had Ed's arm. Daisy kept her hand to her face, and she clung to Walter. Hazel flashed a meaning look to Cora. The girls might not be very badly injured, but they needed help - that sort of help.

"Well!" exclaimed Cora. "You look as if something did happen."

"Oh, I'm all scratched," fluttered Daisy. "That is, my face feels like a grater." She took her handkerchief from the abused face. A few harmless scratches were discernible.

"Not so bad," said Jack. "Just the correct lines, I believe, for - let me see - intellectuality."

"Oh, you needn't joke," snapped Daisy. "I suppose Cecelia - is - badly hurt!"

She said this with the evident intention of drawing attention to Jack's attitude toward Cecilia.

"Now, Daisy," said Jack good-naturedly, "if you want to dump in the ditch again, and will only give me the chance, I will be perfectly delighted to fish you out: I fancy I would get you first shot."

"Oh, you need not bother," interrupted Walter. "I can take care of Miss Bennet."

At this he spread his handkerchief most carefully on the grass, and, with mock concern, assisted Daisy to the low seat.

Ed followed suit, adding to the handkerchief cushion his cap - to make the grass softer for Maud.

"But however did you happen along, Cecilia?" asked Belle, who now added her dainty self to the line of girls on the roadside.

"Now, here!" called Jack. "No more happenings! I beg your pardon, Belle, but we have had such a surfeit of this happening business that we intend, in the language of the poets, to cut it out."

Cecilia gave Jack a grateful glance. Cora broke in promptly with a new thought - to divert attention.

"And you are the girls who wanted `No Boys!'" exclaimed Walter. "I should just like to know what you would have done without us?"

"There! Didn't I tell you?" said Cora. "They are actually claiming the glory of the whole thing. I suppose, Walter, you hired the ram to do the proper thing in initiating the motor girls in the art of touring?"

"Wouldn't he make a hit, though, at some of our college affairs!" exclaimed Ed. "I wonder if we could buy the beast? Here comes the owner now."

The girls looked alarmed. Suppose the farmer should blame them for the disappearance of the ram!

"I'll do the talking," suggested Walter. "If you say anything, Jack, there might be a row."

"Humph!" said Jack. "I suppose you know just how to deal with ram owners."

The farmer was quite up to them now. He was not an ill-natured-looking man, and as he approached he touched his big straw hat.

"No one hurt?" he asked, much to the girls' relief.

"Oh, no, thank you," said Cora, before Walter could open his mouth. "I hope you have not lost the sheep."

"Lose him! Couldn't do that if you chucked him in the mill-pond and let the dam loose on him. Only yesterday the plagued thing went for my wife. Yes, sir, and he 'most knocked her down. When I seed your steam wagons comin' along I knowed there would be trouble. He's that pesky!"

The man looked at the disabled machine.

"Busted?" he asked.

"Some," replied Walter. "But I guess we can manage. Would you like to sell that ram?"

"Sell him? What for? To kill folks as try to feed him? I bought him from a fellow who always wore an overcoat, and, bless me, that ram got so used to it if I haven't had to put my ulster on the hottest days this summer to do down to the pasture where he was chewin'."

The boys laughed heartily at this. Walter seemed keener than ever now on making a bargain.

"Well, you see," he said, "we might use the fellow for stunts - tricks. I think we might train him -"

A scream from Belle startled them.

"Oh!" she yelled. "There he comes! What shall we do?"

Without waiting for instructions, however, Belle, with the other girls, jumped up and started for a little cottage not far from the roadside. The ram was coming over the fields straight for the autos.

"Now wait," cautioned the farmer, as the boys made ready to confront the animal. "Just keep back until he gets near that machine. Then maybe we can git him."

"He's game sport, all right," said Walter. "He evidently hasn't had enough."

The brush and low trees along the road made it possible for the young men to hide, while the excited animal dashed through the tall grass out into the road.

He went straight for the hay wagon. With a bound he was in the decorated auto, like a beast in a cage, with the rack and hay trimmings surrounding him.

"Now we've got him," said the farmer; "that is, if we're careful."

"How?" whispered Ed.

"Someone must lasso him. "The farmer held out the rope in his hand, making a loop ready to throw over the ram's head.

The girls had reached the cottage, but were calling to the boys all sorts of warning and cautions.

"When he gets at the hay," said the farmer, "I guess he'll eat. That run likely whet up his appetite."

"More fun than a deer hunt," said Jack, laughing. "I wonder what will turn up next on this motor girls' tour."

"Get busy," said Ed, creeping toward the hay wagon. "Now, Walter - Oh, Glory be! If he isn't at my four-dollar gloves!"

Quick, like the well=trained athlete that he was, Ed grabbed the rope from the farmer, sprang to the hay rack and made a cast.

It landed true on the animal's horns.

"I've got him!" exclaimed the boy. "Now, fellows, quick! Make his legs fast."

No need to say "quick," for the boys were up and busy making fast the beast before the surprised farmer had a chance to exclaim.

"So you like the real thing in gloves?" asked Ed while pulling at the rope. "Well, I fancy you will make something real -

perhaps a robe - for the best record of this trip. Oh, I say, fellows, let's buy the brute, have him done up properly, and offer his coat to the girl who comes home with a record."

Shouts of glee followed this suggestion, and the girls, seeing that the animal was made safe, were now running back from the cottage to add their voices to the excitement.

Clip insisted upon helping to tie the ram - she declared he had done his share toward making it uncomfortable for her - while Daisy, in her timid way, wanted to do something to the "saucy thing" for upsetting her, and Jack suggested that she "box his horrid ears."

Cora glanced at her watch.

"If it's all the same to the gentlemen," she said, "we will continue on our way. We have lost a full hour already."

"Lost!" repeated Walter meaningly.

"She said `lost,'" faltered Ed with similar intent.

"Not actually lost," corrected Cora, "but at least dropped out of our itinerary."

"We were due ten miles ahead now," sighed Maud in her wistful way.

"Too bad, too bad," whimpered Jack, who was still pulling at the ram's rope. "But it was not our fault, girls. Now, Daisy, do you think you can run your machine without taking in any more circuses? We have examined your car, and it is intact - not so much as a footprint did the naughty beast leave."

Clip was looking over her runabout. It was not damaged, it seemed, and for this she was most grateful. Clip was not out for pleasure - you have guessed that - and it would have been highly inconvenient for that young lady to go back to town in the hay.

Jack left off at the ram's horn, and came to crank up for her.

"All right, Clip?" he asked with evident concern. "I don't want you to go over that lonely road if you do not feel just like it. I can go with you."

"You!" she exclaimed. "Why, Jack Kimball, what are you thinking about?" and she laughed airily. "If you want to finish the impression we started the other day, just take another ride with me. No, Jack, my dear boy, I am very much all right, and very much obliged. But I must hurry off. Whatever will my little brown Wren think of me?" She stepped into the car. "Good-by, girls," she called. "I am so sorry I delayed you, but so glad we met. Take care of the ram, boys, and am I eligible for the trophy? I am a motor girl, you know."

"Of course you are," said Jack, before the others could speak. "All motor girls are eligible."

"Ida Giles, too?" asked Bess. The moment she had spoken she could have bitten her tongue. Why could she never hide her feelings about Jack and Clip?

"And, girls," called Cecilia, who was starting now, "don't forget about your promise. Wren is counting on results."

"What promise?" asked Ed.

"Oh, don't you know?" replied Cora. "Well, I am afraid Jack will have to tell you. We really have not another moment. Are you ready, girls?"

"Why, our strange promise," put in Maud, who was glad to have a "real remark" to make to Ed. "We promised a little girl we would find an old table for her and we have just ransacked the farmer's house, hoping to find it.

Cora burst out laughing. Such an explanation!

"Why, I'll promise a `little girl' that," said Ed, taking up Cora's laugh. "Any qualifications? Might it be a time-table?"

Maud pouted. She stepped into Cora's car, evidently disgusted with boys in general.

Gertrude had something to say to Walter, and was obliged to stand up on the hay rack to do so, as the young man would not let go the rope that held the ram.

There was a sudden hum of an auto, and Clip was gone.

"Thought she had a sick relative," murmured Bess.

"So she has," said Jack, who overheard the remark. "But she came near neglecting her this morning. That was a close call."

"Oh, yes," said Bess with a curled lip. "It seems to me everything Cecilia does is close."

"Bess Robinson!" exclaimed Jack. "Do you want me to hug you? You have been treating me shamefully for weeks past. Now, own up. What have I done?"

Jack knew how to restore Bess to good humor, and his success this time was marked.

"You ridiculous boy!" exclaimed Bess. "You know perfectly well what I mean."

And Jack did.

CHAPTER XIII

AT THE GROTTO

We have dropped something," said Cora as the party started off again.

"Yes," replied Gertrude, "I agree with Ray that the boys are jolly. We miss them already."

"Hush!" cautioned Cora. "We are to have nothing to do with boys on this trip."

She laughed at her own assertion.

"Nothing more to do with them?" asked Belle. Bess kept her machine within talking distance.

"Till the next time," replied Cora, throwing in the second speed gear. "But we will certainly have to hurry now. What on earth do you suppose Walter will do with that ram?"

"What on earth do you think the ram will do with Walter?" replied Ray.

"He paid the farmer three dollars for him, and the man declared he could have him for nothing," said Belle. "Now, that three dollars -"

"Would have bought orchids," interrupted Cora, teasing Belle for her sentimentality.

"Cora," spoke Hazel suddenly, "did you hear what Ed said to Jack about Paul's hold-up?"

"The forbidden topic," interrupted Gertrude. "Hazel, you don't want to lose the sheepskin for insubordination, do you?"

"But, Gertrude, please," begged Hazel quite seriously, "I really must speak to Cora. I will promise not to be blue, but you know I am very anxious about Paul."

"Then speak on, very briefly," replied Gertrude. "I will allow you exactly five minutes."

"Thanks," said Hazel. "Cora," she began again, "Ed told Jack that the papers lost from the mail belonged to Mr. Robinson, and have to do with a very valuable patent. Do you suppose the post-office will do anything to Paul?"

"Oh, you precious baby!" exclaimed Cora. "Don't you know that Paul has been entirely cleared? The mystery is simply who took the papers and otherwise left the mailbag intact?"

"Poor Paul!" sighed the sister.

"Poor Hazel!" added Cora. "A sister who is always worrying about a handsome brother is bound to lose him, eh, Gertrude?"

Gertrude blushed. She had only met Paul once, and at that time her remark was so positive that Cora had seized the opportunity of teasing the girl. That she never noticed boys was Gertrude's claim at college, and now Cora was delighted to have a chance of reversing the claim.

Daisy and Maud, who had been at some distance from the Whirlwind, now cut past Bess and Belle, making their way to the side of the big maroon car.

"Cora," called Daisy, "I forgot to tell you. I found this little satchel by the road where we stopped."

Cora gazed at the black bag that Daisy held up for her inspection.

"Why," faltered Cora, "that must belong to Clip. Why didn't you ask to whom it did belong?"

"I really never thought a word about it until Maud said just now it must be Clip's."

"But why did you pick it up without asking?" insisted Cora, her voice somewhat indignant.

"It was dropped on the road. I thought of course it belonged to some of the girls, and just threw it in my car in a hurry when you called to us to hasten along," said Daisy, her voice sharp and eyes flashing.

"I am sure it must belong to Clip," said Cora, calming down. "I hope it will not inconvenience her."

"I wish you would take the smelly thing," shouted Daisy. "It smells like papa's office, and I hate drugs."

"Clip was going to see some sick relative," went on Cora, "and of course the satchel -"

"Must be filled with the sickness," and Daisy laughed sarcastically. "Well, papa's bag smells that way, but he has more than one `sick relative.' "

Cora frowned. Gertrude looked surprised. Hazel shook her head at Daisy.

"Toss it here," called Cora. "I just love disinfectants."

Daisy threw the bag into the Whirlwind. Then she put on

speed and passed the big car.

For a few miles the girls seemed very quiet, scarcely any conversation being held.

It was but a short run to the Grotto, the little wayside tea-house. The party was a full hour late, but Cora knew she could depend upon generous excuses for the motor girls.

So many things might happen by the way, and so many things did happen.

"I suppose," murmured Ray, "the biscuit will be stony. I do love hot biscuit."

"Don't worry. Tillie will keep things hot, if she possibly can do so. But I hear they have had some very busy days at the Grotto. I hope we have not hit upon the very busiest. Gertrude, have I told you about the Grotto? Did you know that Mathilde Herold and Adele Genung are keeping a tea-house this summer, to earn enough money for their senior year? And they have done surprisingly well. Yes, their folks have a summer place near the tea-house, so the girls go home nights, and of course the place must be very pretty - Tillie is an artist in decorating."

"Splendid!" exclaimed Gertrude. "Of course I know Tillie. What girl at Springsley doesn't know her? She has been decorating for every affair at the gym. And she always helped with chapel. Oh, yes, indeed, Cora, I agree with you, Tillie Herold is an artist."

"Well, let us hope her talent is not confined to mere walls," said Ray. "Hot biscuit requires a different stroke, I believe."

"In accepting us for to-day," said Cora. "Tillie stipulated that we should dine table d'hote and no questions asked. I hope, Ray, you will not be disappointed."

"Oh, there they are!" exclaimed Hazel. "I see some one waving her apron!"

"That's Adele," replied Cora. "She knows how to wave aprons. Don't you remember, Gertrude, the night she served the Welsh rarebit, when she made an apron of our best table-piece with a string through the middle?"

Cora turned her auto to the roadside. Then she called to the cars following:

"Here we are, girls. Get your machines well in from the road."

"Oh, what a charming place!" exclaimed Belle, who was not slow to observe the attractions of the little Grotto. It seemed all porch and vines, one of those picture places, ample for an eating house, but unsuited for anything else.

"There!" gasped Daisy; "that's the sort of house to live in!"

"To live out of, you mean," put in Maud. "I can't see how one could live `in' there."

The cars were all motionless now. Cora and Gertrude had already "escaped" from the college hug of Adele and Tillie. When the Chelton girls had been introduced, the vine-covered porch was actually filled with the members of the motor party.

"How splendid!" exclaimed Tillie, with that delightful German accent that defies letters and requires a pretty mouth to "exhale."

"Darling!" went on Adele, with all the extravagance of schoolgirl enthusiasm.

"You leave us no adjectives," remarked Cora. "I never saw anything so sweet. How ever did you get those vines to grow so promptly?"

"Wild cucumber," said Adele with a laugh, "Why, you know, dear, wild cucumber can no more help growing than you can. Isn't she tall, Tillie? I do believe you have grown inches since school, Cora."

"Yes, mother bemoans it. My duds are all getting away from me."

"And we have been waiting lunch for you ladies. I did hope we would not have a single visitor to-day, so that we might entertain you properly," went on Adele, "but two horrid men called. Wanted 'tea'; but indeed I know what they wanted - just a quiet place to talk about their old patent papers."

"Yes, and one broke a beautiful china cup," said Tillie.

"But he had his thumb gone," Adele hurried to say. "I saw him directly I went to pick up the pieces. So I suppose we could not exactly blame the man for dropping Tillie's real German cup."

"His thumb gone!" repeated Cora absently.

"Oh!" exclaimed Hazel. "The man we met after Paul's hold-up had lost a joint of his thumb."

"And papa said the papers stolen were patent papers!" exclaimed Bess, all excitement.

"Hush!" whispered Belle. "Bess, you know father particularly said we were not to speak of that."

If, as is claimed, the mature woman has the wonderful advantage of an instinct almost divine, then the growing girl has, undoubtedly, the advantage of intuitive shocks - flashes of wireless insight into threatening surroundings.

Such a flash was distinctly felt now through the Grotto - even the two young proprietors, who were not supposed to be really concerned, felt distinctly that "something was doing somewhere."

Cora sank down into a low wicker chair. Bess and Belle managed to both get upon a very small divan, while Daisy, Maud and Ray, the "three graces," stood over in the corner, where an open window let in just enough honeysuckle to sift the very sofest possible sunshine about the group.

But Hazel lingered near the telephone. She had confided to Cora that Paul was not at all well when he left home in the morning, and just now she was wondering if it would seem silly for her to call up the Whitehall Company and ask to speak with her brother.

At that instant the telephone bell rang.

It sent the expected shock through the little assemblage, and Cora jumped up as if she anticipated a message.

Tillie took down the receiver.

Presently she was saying "no" and "yes," and then she repeated Cora's name.

She handed the receiver to Cora with a whispered word.

Hazel's face went very white.

"You little goose!" exclaimed Bess, who instantly noticed the change. "Is there no one here worth a telephone message but Hazel Hastings?"

"Yes, Ed - Ed Foster," they heard Cora say. Then she listened a long time. Her face did not betray pleasure, and her words were plainly disguised.

"All right, Ed," she said finally. "I will attend to it at once. Oh, yes, a perfectly lovely time. Thank you - we are just about to dine. Good-by."

Cora was slow to hang up the receiver. And when she turned around Hazel Hastings confronted her.

"Oh, is it Paul?" asked Hazel. "Tell me quickly. What has happened to Paul?"

"Hazel," said Cora, "you must have your lunch. You are dreadfully excitable."

But it was Cora Kimball who was distracted, who played with her lunch without apparent appetite, and it was she who could take but one cup of tea in the fascinating little tea-house, the college girls' Grotto.

CHAPTER XIV

THE PROMISE BOOK LOST

Now, Cora, dear," began Gertrude, in her quiet, yet convincing way, "you may just as well tell us what you are waiting for. We are guessing all sorts of things, and the truth cannot possibly be as bad."

They were sitting on the porch of the Grotto, and although they were away behind scheduled time at that point, Cora insisted she wanted to rest a bit, and seemed loath to move.

Cora Kimball tired after twenty-five miles! As well accuse the Whirlwind of drinking its own gasoline.

Hazel was almost feverish. Cora had not divulged the purport of the telephone message, beyond admitting it was from Ed, which gave Ray the chance for her little joke on the combination of names - Cora and Ed, the "Co-Eds."

"When the Co-Eds conspire," lisped Ray, "we may as well wait patiently. We will have to wait their pleasure, of course."

Cora did not mind the sarcasm. She was certainly not like herself. Bess and Belle were even anxious about her, and offered all sorts of remedies, from bicarbonate of soda to dry tea.

"Now," said Cora finally, "it is two o'clock. Do you really

think we ought to make Breakwater tonight?"

"Why not?" gasped Daisy. "Won't Aunt May be waiting for us? And it is only thirty miles."

"Yes, but," faltered Cora, "suppose you should have a breakdown on that lonely road? There is neither station nor house from here to the falls."

"What should break down?" asked Daisy. "This is papa's best machine, if you mean it is not trustworthy."

"Oh, Daisy, dear, I had no idea of insinuating such a thing. Your machine, of course, is just as trustworthy as any of the others. But I was thinking how delightful it would be to spend the night here. I really must confess to being broken up by that ram accident," and Cora shivered slightly.

The girls looked at her in astonishment. Her words did not ring true; Cora Kimball was a poor actress.

"If Cora wants to stay," said Tillie, "I should think you would all agree. Cora is captain, is she not?"

"But our trip will be spoiled," wailed Maud. "I do wish I had never come."

"Oh, if there is going to be real distress about it," said Cora, evidently trying hard to pull herself together, "I suppose we had best start. But remember, I have warned you. I have a premonition that we will `run up against' something before night."

"Then I am not going," declared Hazel. "I won't stir one step. Cora, let the others go; you can overtake them with your fast car, and we will meet them in the morning."

This brought on a veritable storm of protest and dissatisfaction. Cora left the girls on the porch, and went outside with Tillie.

"Could you hear anything those men were saying?" she asked the pretty little German. "Were they discussing a patent, do you think?"

"Oh, no; it was not like that," replied Tillie. "It was about - let me see. Some Haster, no, like a name - like your friend's name, Hazel Hastings. That was it, Hastings."

"Did they say Hazel?" pressed Cora.

"No, not that, of course," and Tillie laughed.

"How should they know Hazel? It was a similar name - just Hastings."

"And they unfolded blueprints? Like our campus maps, you know?"

"Yes, they had blue maps; I saw them when I picked up my shattered cup. - It is all very well for Adele to blame his thumb; I blame him - he is too fat, and thinks himself very smart."

Tillie pouted. Evidently her caller had not been too polite, perhaps he had mistaken her for an ordinary waitress.

A distant "honk-honk" startled the girls. Cora rushed out to the road, and before the others knew what she was about she was in conversation with Ed Foster. So quickly did he run up to the Grotto in Jack's car that no one but Cora realized who he was until the machine was stopped and he was out beside her. There was a stranger with him -a business-like looking man. He did not leave the car.

"There!" exclaimed Ray. "Didn't I tell you? It was this Co-Ed business that kept her. Cora can't fool me."

"Hazel," said Cora, stepping up to the porch, "Ed thinks you had best not go on with us. Paul is not well - he is not very sick, though -"

Hazel turned white, and Cora put her arm around her. "Now you must not be frightened. It is nothing serious, and I will go back with you," she said.

"Indeed you shall not!" exclaimed Hazel, now calling up all her courage, and proving herself to be the girl she really could be in an emergency. "I shall go back with Ed, if I may."

The girls glanced from one to the other. They understood this was an emergency, that Hazel had been called back to her sick brother, yet with girlish curiosity some of them, at least, showed surprise that Hazel should offer to ride back with Ed Foster.

"But I am not going back," said Ed; "at least not until we - this gentleman and I - have followed the trail a little farther. You see, girls, we are out on a `bear hunt.'"

But the girls did not see - only Cora looked as if she understood. She said to Hazel:

"There is no hurry, dear. You can go with them when they come back. They have to pass this way, don't you, Ed?"

"Would you mind, Cora," said Ed suddenly, "if the gentleman outside asked you a few private questions?"

"A reporter!" exclaimed Ray, all excitement.

"Dear me! I do hope he won't ask for our pictures. Mother would never permit it."

Ed smiled broadly. He looked a sort of assent, but did not otherwise express it.

Cora stepped up to the auto, whereat the man left his place, and, under pretext of walking along idly, and perhaps thus gaining Cora's "private ear," he was soon out of reach of those on the porch.

"It is like a double robbery," he said after exchanging some preliminary remarks, "and the child is disconsolate. Her mother is sure it was not stolen, but lost, while we feel otherwise. It seems there is a handsome young man, a cousin of the child's, interested. His father is a lawyer - the lawyer who has the case against Mr. Robinson. Now this book - the promise book - contained the names of those who visited the cottage on the day that the papers were taken out of the mailbag. It is comparatively easy to guess the sequence."

"You mean they might call on those whose names appear in the book?" asked Cora, beginning to see something of the complex situation.

"Yes, and more than that. They would obtain valuable information from that little book - a clear description of the missing table. If they can find it they will be able to keep the property where it is now - in the possession of Rob Roland, Wren Salvey's rival cousin."

"Rob Roland!" exclaimed Cora. "Why, he was in the party at Robinson's the other evening. He was even attentive to a friend of ours."

"To whom, may I ask?" inquired the detective politely.

"A Miss Thayer, a young student," she replied.

"Miss Thayer! I heard her name mentioned in court this morning. Is she a friend of yours?"

"Yes, indeed!" exclaimed Cora, now alarmed. "What could be said of Cecilia Thayer?"

"Why, she has been on very intimate terms with the Salvey

child, and lawyers devise all sorts of schemes, you know, to meet their own ends. It was hinted that Miss Thayer might know where the missing promise book was."

"Clip take that from Wren! Impossible!" cried Cora. "Oh, this is all a mistake! I must go back. I cannot go on and let Clip be blamed for stealing the promise book."

CHAPTER XV

ROB ROLAND

"Cora Kimball!"

Ed Foster stood up every inch of his height. He was always tall, but now, facing the girl whose name he had so vehemently spoken, he seemed a veritable giant. Cora wanted to be firm; she meant exactly what she said when she declared she would abandon the tour of the motor girls, and go back to Chelton to help Cecilia Thayer out of her difficulty.

But, after all, Cora was only a girl, and Ed was a great, strong man - he ought to know.

"If you cannot trust me, Cora, and allow me to help Clip, I really think you are not doing justice to Jack's friend."

Cora laughed a little. Ed put things so nicely. He never presumed upon her own intimacy - it was always just "Jack's friend."

"Besides," he pressed, seeing, in, Cora's eyes, his advantage, "I feel I can do more alone. I have got to take Hazel back to her brother, then I promise you I shall not rest until I have found Clip, and made sure of her exact situation."

"Oh, I know, Ed, you will do everything possible. But it seems like treason for me to go on a pleasure trip and leave two very dear friends in such trouble. Even Jack may be implicated."

Ed turned away to hide his own tell-tale face. He knew perfectly well that Jack was implicated, knew that Rob Roland had deliberately accused him of taking Cecilia Thayer out to the Salvey cottage for the purpose of gaining possession of the promise book. For this very reason Ed wanted Cora to go on – to escape, if possible, the anxiety she must experience if she should have to know the real story.

"Well," sighed Cora, "it is getting late. I suppose it will be best, Ed, as you say. Take Hazel back, and find Clip. Have her 'phone me at Breakwater, tomorrow."

"That's the girl!" exclaimed Ed, taking both her hands in his own strong clasp. "See, the girls are looking at us. They think you have accepted me."

"I have," she answered, "accepted you, and your terms. Good luck, Ed. It is so nice for Jack to have such a good friend."

Hazel was soon tucked in the little runabout, the detective going on in another car that was sent out to him in answer to his call over the telephone.

"Is your premonition all fulfilled, Cora?" asked Daisy, her voice far from merry. "I suppose you were 'premonited' that Hazel should go off like that."

"If we keep on losing," said Gertrude, "we will soon all fit in the Whirlwind."

Cora stood gazing after the runabout - Jack's car. Hazel's eyes had burned their look upon Cora's face - those deep, violet eyes always seem like live volcanoes, thought Cora.

And Ed - his eyes had been searching, his look - well, it was convincing, that is all Cora would admit even to her own heart.

She turned finally to those on the porch.

"Well," exclaimed Belle, the sentimental one, "who is star-gazing, now? Cora, what did you forget in that runaway car?"

Cora smiled. She had been remiss, and she owed it to the girls to see that their trip was a success. She would atone now.

"Tillie," she said suddenly, "couldn't you and Adele shut up shop for a week and come with us? You have been working hard all summer, and you have made up the required pennies. Now, don't you think it would be perfectly splendid to take the run with us?"

Every one instantly agreed that this would be the very thing, and in spite of the hesitation of Adele and Tillie, who argued that it might not be agreeable to bring strangers into the homes where others had been expected, it was finally settled that the party should wait until the next morning, when the tea-house girls would be ready to start off with them.

Nor were the arrangements without a certain happy possibility - there were two other girls waiting to take up that same little Grotto - to earn college money, as had Tillie and Adele.

"Rena and Margaret will be here first thing in the morning," announced Adele, after her telephone talk with Rena, "and they are perfectly delighted. Oh, isn't it just splendid!"

Then Cora had messages to send. She called up Jack, but only got the maid in answer. She called up Walter, and he also was out. Finally she called up Ed. She waited until she felt he would be at his dinner quarters, and she was not disappointed in getting his own voice in reply.

He told her that everything was all right - that Clip was with little Wren, who had been very ill since the loss of her book, and that Paul Hastings was no worse. This last Cora considered evasive, but had to be content, for Ed would give no more definite information.

Such demands as were made upon that little tea-house telephone that evening! Every one of the girls called up her own home, besides calling up many relatives at the other end of the line, those with whom the tourists expected to visit during the trip.

The Grotto was well situated for business, being about half way between two country seats, and the same distance between two large cities.

"We will close exactly at sundown to-night," said Adele, when a lady from Bentley, who stopped every evening for a cup of tea on her way from the village, had been served.

"Do let me keep shop for a while," begged Cora. "I would just love to be in real business. Mother declares I have a bent for trade. Let me try, Tillie, while you and Adele go over to the cottage and get your things together."

Thus it was that one hour later Cora Kimball was left the sole possessor of the Grotto; every other motor girl managed to either go for a walk, or go with some one who wanted to take a walk, but Cora was glad - she felt the need of rest which only solitude can give.

She sat on the porch; the gentle evening breeze made incense through the honeysuckle. It was delightfully resting; she could hear the voices of the girls in the meadow, after cowslips, buttercups, daisies and clover. They would fetch back a huge bunch, Cora knew, and they would discard them at the steps of the Grotto, as most girls do - run wild for wild flowers, then toss them away when the run is over.

"I hardly think I shall have any business," thought Cora, "although I would just love to wait on somebody."

The rumble of an approaching automobile caught her ear.

"There!" she thought; "the driver of that car may want a sip of Russian tea - I am glad it is not Turkish - that the girls serve here."

The car was almost up to the sycamore tree, just at the side of the Grotto.

Yes, the driver was stopping.

Cora rocked nervously in the wicker chair.

Who would it be? The girls should not have gone so far away -

A young man alighted from the runabout. He stepped briskly up to the porch.

It was Rob Roland.

"Well!" he exclaimed, plainly as surprised to see Cora as she was to see him. "If this isn't luck! Miss Kimball!"

Quick and keen as was his glance, making sure that Cora was alone, her own sharp wits were able to follow his.

"Yes," she replied indifferently, "the girls have closed up the tea-room, and are just out in the meadow. I felt more like sitting here."

He drew up a chair and sat down uninvited. Cora never did like Rob Roland, now she disliked him.

"You are the very person I am most anxious to talk to," he began, "and this is an excellent opportunity."

"About what, pray?" asked Cora. "I must go with the girls very soon."

"Oh, no, you must not," he replied, and, handsome though he was, there was that in his manner that deepened the very lines nature had done her best with, and his eyes were merely smoldering depths.

Cora felt she should not betray the least nervousness, for, though Rob Roland was known to be a gentleman, he might take advantage of her helplessness to gain from her some information. Ed had warned her to beware of him.

"Of course you know all about Cissy Thayer," he began. Cora resented his insolence, but dared not show it. "You know how she has been getting around my little cousin, the cripple."

Cora glared at him. She felt that his cowardly attack was simply a display of weakness, and she knew a coward is easily overcome. She deliberately drew her chair closer to him.

"Rob Roland," she said calmly, "my friend, Miss Thayer, is not only a lady, but she is also a student of human ills. She has been interested in little Wren that she might be cured. It appears that some of her relatives consider her incurable."

"Cured!" he sneered. "That misfit made right! Why, she has only a few months to live. Your friend is very foolish. She should put her energy on something worth while. And she should be careful how she handles their property. That scrapbook, for instance."

"How dare you, Rob Roland!" exclaimed Cora. "Miss Thayer says the child has been ill-treated through alleged treatment, and it appears the man who has been treating her was paid by your father."

"Oh, my!" The fellow sank deeper into his linen coat. "I had no idea of your dramatic powers, Miss Kimball. I beg a thousand pardons. I never dreamed that the Thayer girl was so close to you. In fact, I rather thought you merely took her up out of charity. Every one in Chelton knows that the Thayers are just poor working-people."

That was too much for Cora. She stepped to the door of the tea-room with dismissal in her manner. He knew she intended him to leave at once.

"But what I want to know," he said, deliberately following her, "is just who this Thayer girl is. It is important that we should know, to go on with the -"

"We!" interrupted Cora. "Pray, who are `we'?"

"Why, my father's firm, the lawyers, you know," he stammered. "Some day, Miss Kimball, I expect to represent the firm of Roland, Reed & Company."

Cora turned and looked at him. It was on that very spot that she had turned to Ed - Ed was so like this young man, the same dark, handsome youth, and just about his age.

But Ed was, after all, so different - so very different.

Cora was gaining time as she strove to hold him by her magnetic glance. Any youth would accept it; he did not despise it.

"Mr. Roland," she said, in her own inimitable velvet tones, "you are making a very great mistake. If you really believe that Cecilia Thayer had anything to do with the loss of that child's book, you are wrong; if you think she had any other than humane motives in visiting the child, you are wrong again. Cecilia Thayer -"

"Oh, now come, Cora," he interrupted. "You don't mind me calling you Cora? I know the whole scheme. Your brother Jack is - well, he is quite clever, but not clever enough to cover up his tracks." He grasped Cora's arm and actually dragged her to him. "Don't you know that Cissy Thayer and Jack Kimball are suspected of abduction? That Wren Salvey has been stolen-stolen, do you hear?"

CHAPTER XVI

A STRANGE MESSAGE

Uproarious laughter from the girls with the wild flowers aroused Cora. Rob Roland was gone.

Had she fainted? Was that roaring in her ears just awakened nerves?

"Cora! Oh, Cora! We had the most darling time," Bess was bubbling. "You should have been along. Such a dear old farmer. He showed us the queerest tables. And he had the nicest son. Cora - What is the matter?"

"Oh," lisped Ray, "another Co-Ed message over the telephone."

"Cora, dear," exclaimed Gertrude, "we should not have left you all alone. Are you ill?"

"Cora! Cora!" gasped Adele.

"Cora, dear!" sighed Tillie.

"Oh, Cora!" moaned Belle. "What has happened?"

"Cora, darling," cried Maud, "who has frightened you?"

"Cora Kimball," called Daisy, "have you been drinking too

much tea?"

"Too little," murmured Cora. "Will some of you girls leave off biting the air, and make a good cup of tea?"

There was a wild rush for the alcohol lamp; every one wanted to make the good cup of tea.

"I saw a runabout moving away as we came up," said Ray. "I hope, Cora, your caller was not obnoxious."

"Oh, just an autoist," replied Cora indifferently. "I did not take the trouble to brew tea for one solitary man." The color was coming back into her cheeks now, and with the return of animation her scattered senses attempted to seize upon the strange situation.

Jack and Clip to be arrested for abduction!

Could that fellow have known what he was saying?

If only Jack would call her up on the telephone. She had left word for him to do so, no matter how late the hour might be when he should return home.

"Now drink every sip of this," commanded Adele, as she turned on the lights and fetched Cora a steaming cup of the very best Grotto Hyson. "There is nothing for shaken nerves better than perfectly fresh tea, and, you see, we make it without soaking the leaves."

"It is delightful," said Cora, sipping the savory draught. "I must learn how to make tea this way - it is so different from the home-brewed variety."

Gertrude sat close to the reclining girl. "Is there nothing I can do, Cora?" she asked. "No message I can send?"

"Yes," whispered Cora; "you can manage to get the girls out of here before you and I leave for the night. I want to use the telephone privately."

Gertrude understood. She had not been a roommate with Cora Kimball for two years without knowing something of her temperament. She pressed her friend's hand gently, then said loud enough for the others to hear:

"We will soon have to get our machines under cover. Tillie says her grandfather has all sorts of sheds over around his country place. In fact, he has a regular shed-farm. Cora, I am just dying to try running a motor. Would you trust me to get the Whirlwind in the shed safely?"

"Of course I would, Gertrude," and Cora jumped up from the wicker divan. "I would suggest that some one go along, though - perhaps Ray. She has had some experience, and you know the Whirlwind"

"Is not a prize-package machine," interrupted Gertrude. "All right, Cora. I will humbly take instructions. Come along, girls. It will be dark directly, and then we might have to waste time lighting the lamps."

"And grandfather's man has offered to look over every machine early in the morning," said Tillie. "He is quite expert; we will be sure that every nut and bolt is in perfect order."

This was good news to the motor girls, especially to Daisy, who had her own secret doubts about her father's best car - she was accustomed to running the substitute.

Presently all except Cora and Adele were attending to the cars. Cora was just about to call up her own house when the tinkle of the telephone bell startled her. She picked up the receiver and was not surprised to find the party inquired for was herself.

"This is Jack," came the welcome voice. "Is that you, sis?"

"Oh, yes, Jack, dear!" she replied. Adele had gone out to fetch the chairs in from the porch. "I have been almost frantic. Where are you? Where is Clip? Where is Wren?"

"Oh, easy there, now, sis," and Cora thought she had never before appreciated the value of a real brother. "I can't answer everything at once, although I can come pretty near it. First, I am here - at home. Next, Clip is here - at our home, and third, the other party - I won't mention names - is here also."

"All at our house?" exclaimed Cora.

And the answer came: "Exactly that. But you mustn't say a word to any one. You know, there has been a sort of rumpus. Do you want to speak with C.? She is here."

"Hello, Cora," came Cecilia's voice. "How are you? Not getting on with your trip very fast, I guess."

"Oh, Clip!" said Cora. "I cannot understand it -"

"You are not supposed to," replied the other. "We are all right, you are all right, and what more do you ask?"

"How is Paul?"

"Well, he did have quite a time, but is improving. Say, Cora," and the voice was subdued, "don't call us up until you hear from me. I can't explain now. But where shall I write - say in two days' time?"

"Two days!" repeated Cora. "Do you expect me to exist that long and not know -"

"I am afraid you will have to. We are being watched" - this was barely breathed - "and a break would spoil it all. Surely you can trust me."

The girls were coming back-were actually on the porch. Cora

was obliged to say a few disconnected words, and then she hung up the receiver.

CHAPTER XVII

THE ROAD TO BREAKWATER

"What a delightful morning!" exclaimed Maud. "The wait was certainly worth while. I do believe there is something inspiring about the morning air."

"Yes," rejoined Daisy, throwing in the second speed, "it always makes me feel like a human rain-barrel. I want to go out in a great, big field, and sit down in a lump. Then I want to throw back my head and open my mouth very wide. That is my idea of drinking in the fresh morning air."

"Well, never mind the dewy morning business," called Cora. "Just get your machines well under way. You know, we must make twenty-five miles by noon."

Cora was, as usual, in the lead. Daisy and Maud came next, then Bess and Belle lined up the rear, as Cora thought it best that the two big machines should lead and trail.

Cora tried her best to be cheerful. She had definite ideas about a friend's duty to a friend, and no one could say she failed in that duty. Why should she think of Jack and Clip and Wren when she was captain of the Motor Girls' Club, and they expected a good time on their initial run?

"Oh, I am so glad everything happened!" exclaimed Tillie, who was in the Whirlwind; "for if everything did not happen we never could have come along."

"And we never could have had all our camping things," put in Gertrude. "I am just dying to get out on the grass and light up under the kettles. That was a very bright idea of Adele's to fetch along part of the tea-house outfit."

"Won't it be jolly to build miniature caves to keep the wind from the lamp?" suggested Cora. "I tell you, after all, the motor girls were poor housekeepers - we had to take lessons from our business friends."

This pleased Tillie immensely. She was the sort of girl who is glad to prove a theory, and in keeping the tea-house she had proven that girls - mere girls - are not always sawdust dolls.

Daisy was speeding up her machine to speak with Cora.

"There's Cedar Grove over there!" she shouted; "and Aunt May's is only four miles from the turn in the road."

"But we are going to lunch on the road," replied Cora. "The girls are bent on camping out."

A cloud fell over Daisy's sensitive face. "I must telephone to papa that I am all right," she remarked. "Aunt May expected us last night, and if you girls do not want to come, Maud and I will go. We can meet you farther on."

"Oh, of course," Cora hurried to say, "we must go on, since we are expected. We can have the camping out to-morrow. I had actually lost track of our plans in the mix-up."

"Isn't it too bad that Hazel had to turn back?" said Ray. "I do hope her brother is not seriously ill."

"I heard last night that he was very much better," replied Cora. "It seems that robbery unnerved him. Ridiculous as the situation appeared, it was no fun to Paul. I don't wonder he broke down."

Bess, Belle and Adele were in the Flyaway, and they, like the others, seemed to take new pleasure in flying over the roads since they had realized what it meant to have to stand still.

Adele was all enthusiasm. She had not often been privileged to enjoy automobile sport, and the prospect of the trip seemed like an unopened wonder book to her - every mile revealed new delights.

Along the shady byways, through the Numberland Hills, past the famous springs, where everybody stopped to drink and make a wish, the motor girls took their way.

"Let me lead now, Cora?" asked Daisy. "I am just dying for Aunt May to see us come up. And say, girls, I've got the dearest, darlingest cousin - a young doctor!"

A scream went up from every throat. Daisy had not told of her attractive cousin until the party were within very sight of him.

"Me first!" shouted Belle. "I have been a perfect angel ever since we left Chelton; didn't even speak to the nice man with the short thumb - Clip's friend."

At that moment an auto dashed by. Tillie seized Cora's arm.

"That's the man who talked about Hastings!" she exclaimed. "The man who took tea in our house yesterday."

"And that's the very man we met on the road the day Paul was help up," Cora declared. "Oh, now I see the coincidence. Of course they heard of the hold-up, they being on the road about the time it happened, and when they were at your house they might have been discussing the latest account of the affair - there was something in the daily paper about it, you know."

Cora was not sure she believed herself, but at the moment she decided it would be best for the happiness of the party to think lightly of the meeting with the strange men. Rob Roland's voice still rang in her ears like a threat, and while she was no coward neither did she invite trouble.

There seemed now to be clearly some connection between the missing papers from the mailbag and the missing promise book, but of the two Cora's girlish heart considered the loss of the book the more serious.

"Did you ever see such old-fashioned houses in all your born days?" asked Bess. "Look at that one over there. If our table is not in that house, then we had better abandon the antique and look in some new, first-class hotel."

"That house over there is my aunt's!" shouted Daisy, laughing at Bess for making the blunder, "and I am going to tell Duncan exactly what you have said about it."

Bess begged off, and made all sorts of apologies, but Daisy insisted that her cousin, the doctor, should hear what Bess thought of one of the finest old mansions in Breakwater.

"Here we are!" called Daisy, pulling up on the gravel drive. "And there are Duncan and Aunt May."

Out on the broad veranda stood a young man - plainly a professional, for while at a glance a girl might decide that Duncan Bennet was "up to date," still there was about him that disregard for conventionality that betokens high thinking, with no room for the consideration of trifling details of every-day life.

Cora instantly said: "There! He's fine!"

Ray was thinking: "How unpolished!"

Bess whispered to Belle: "I see trouble ahead. Gertrude will want to take him along."

Maud was "adjusting her eyes." She could not forget her famous "imploring look."

But Duncan Bennet, with one bound, left the veranda, clearing the steps without touching them, and he was in front of Daisy's car dangerously soon.

"Look out, Duncan!" called Daisy. "Do you want to spatter yourself all over my nice clean machine?"

"Not exactly," he replied, "but I felt I should do something definite to welcome you. I suppose I may extend the kiss of peace?"

"Oh!" gasped Maud. "Will he really kiss us?"

"Without a doubt," replied his cousin, laughing. "Duncan Bennet is famous for his hospitality, and quite demonstrative. Don't worry, dear. He is an awfully nice fellow."

CHAPTER XVIII

THE CLUE

Jack Kimball sat in his study, with his hands laced in his thick, dark hair. He was thinking - Jack claimed the happy faculty of being able to think of one thing at a time, and to do that thoroughly.

Suddenly he jumped up, and, whistling a tune that only a happy youth knows how to originate, he dashed up the polished stairs, three steps at a time, and finally reached the third floor of his home.

He was met in the hall by a matronly woman with a tray in her hands, and at his approach she stepped back to allow him to enter a room, the door of which was swung open.

"Morning, Miss Brown," he said. "How's the baby?"

"Doing splendidly, thank you," replied the woman, "and she is very anxious to see you. Won't you step in?"

"Sure thing," answered Jack. "That's just what I came up for. I want to chat with her myself."

He stepped lightly into the apartment. It was plainly furnished, with a keen appreciation of what was needed in a sick room, and what should be left out of it. Jack sank into a steamer chair beside the white bed.

"How are things, Wren?" he asked, stroking the delicate hand that was put out to greet him. "Are you almost strong enough to - play football?"

The child smiled, and turned her head away. She had never known any one in all her life like Jack Kimball, so big and strong, and yet so kind. He almost made her feel timid and shy.

"I'm better every minute," she managed to say. "But, of course, I ought to be."

She glanced at her nurse, Miss Brown, who was bringing the morning's beef tea.

"She is really doing splendidly," put in the nurse. "But she is a model patient - never wants what is not good for her."

"Is Clip coming to-day?" asked Wren, hesitating as she said "Clip."

"I hope so," replied Jack, "but you know she is very busy, and may not get here. But if she does not" - noting the child's disappointment - "she will surely come to-morrow. She telephoned so last night."

"Did she say anything about the book?" queried the little one.

"That's exactly what I want to talk about," he replied with nice evasion. "I wonder are you well enough to try to remember about that book. Where did you last have it?"

"Out in my chair, with mother. I asked a little boy along the road to hand me some flowers, the book slipped back of me, and, as mother wheeled me along, I could feel that it was all right. When we got home it was gone."

"And you didn't speak with any other persons than this boy?" Jack continued.

"Oh, there were a lot of people out to see the firemen's parade, and lots of them spoke to me."

"But did any one walk along with you to talk with you?"

"Yes," she said with hesitation, trying to recall that day's momentous happenings; "there were two people. They were strangers. I think they had been in an automobile, for the girl was dressed like a motor girl, and the young man wore a long duster."

Jack stopped and made a mental note of this remark. He had evidently expected this intelligence.

"What did they look like - I mean personally?"

"The girl had red hair - I particularly noticed that," replied the child; "but I have no idea what the man looked like, for he walked back of my chair."

"I'm not tiring her, am I, Miss Brown?" asked Jack, turning to the nurse. "I can wait for the other details."

"Go right on," assented the woman, who was dressed in the garb of a nurse. "I think the talk will do her good; she has been so anxious about it all."

"And these two people talked with you?" pursued Jack.

"Why, yes. The girl sat down on the roadside, and mother stopped my chair. Let me see; I think mother went into the little candy shop and left them with me. They were very pleasant. I am sure they would never touch my book."

"Did you tell them what it was?"

"I did, of course. I always told everybody what my precious book was. I asked them to sign my promise, and they both did so."

"Oh!" exclaimed Jack, whistling his punctuation. "They did sign, did they?"

"Why, I thought you knew that," replied Wren. "But I did not see the book after they signed, so I do not know their names. You see, mother was in a hurry, and they just gave me the book and - Oh, what could have become of my precious book!" she broke off, her voice like a cry from her very heart.

"Well, now there!" soothed Jack. "I knew I should not have distressed you about it. But, you see, I had to know, else I could not find it. Now I feel I shall have it back to you in jig time. Brace up, little girl"; and he tried to impart both courage and hope by his manner. "Don't you know you are sure to get some wonderful blessing for having to stand this loss? That's Cora's pet theory. She almost drives a fellow after trouble declaring he will find joy at his heels."

Wren was sighing. Her book had been to her so much. More, perhaps, than some animal pet is to the average cripple, both companion and distraction.

Miss Brown brought the bottle of alcohol, and bathed the child's temples.

"Do you know, Mr. Kimball," she said, "we have a secret for you. Wren stood up yesterday!"

"Bully for the legs!" cried Jack, with an absolute disregard of the way he was expressing his joy. The remark brought the color bark to Wren's cheeks.

"Yes," breathed Wren; "but they - my feet - are awfully full of pins and needles."

"Save them, save them," went on Jack. "I can never find a pin in this house. Cora fainted one day, and the doctor said it was pins. He had to take out twenty pins to give her back her breath."

"I wish your sister were home," said Wren, looking wistfully out of the low window beside the bed. "She is so like Clip - and Clip can't be here."

"She'll be home soon, all right," replied Jack, who was now standing at the door, "and when she does come we will all know it. Cora Kimball is a brass and a lawn mower, rolled into one piece. You should be glad she is away," he finished, his words actually accusing himself of falsehood.

"Fetch her, and let me see," spoke Wren, trying to appear as cheerful as she, had been when her visitor entered her room.

"Well, I'll fetch something next time," he replied. "If I can't get Cora or Clip I'll get - ice cream."

CHAPTER XIX

PAUL AND HAZEL

Meanwhile, at another bed of sickness sat a girl pale and wan from nights and days of anxiety. Hazel Hastings had left the motor girls' tour and hurried to her sick brother with more apprehension stirring her heart than the report of his actual condition warranted. Paul had always been subject to peculiar spells - shocks they were termed - but Hazel knew what collapse meant, or what it might mean, unless -

Brother and sister were to each other what the whole world might be to others. Paul had kept up well under the strain of the hold-up, but when suspicion was pointed at him he collapsed.

Who could be at the back of the defaming scheme to spread the report? Who could have dared to say that he was in league with whoever took those papers from the mailbag?

"Are you better, Paul?" murmured the girl. "You had a lovely sleep."

"Oh, yes," he sighed. "I feel almost good. If only my head would stop throbbing. What time is it?"

"Almost noon, dear, and Clip will soon be here."

"Will she fetch the morning papers? I must see how the thing is going on. They were to go to court this morning."

"Now you must not think of that, you know, Paul," commanded the girl gently. "If you are to grow strong enough to go and take your own part you will have to leave the others alone. There is nothing new, or I should have told you."

"But Mr. Robinson called - I heard you talking to him last night."

"Yes, you did, dear. But he came to inquire for you. He is very anxious about you."

Hazel Hastings went to the dresser and slipped under the cover a piece of yellow paper. Paul was getting better, and he should not see Mr. Robinson's check for money, which that gentleman had insisted upon leaving for the sick boy's expenses. They were not poor, neither were they rich, but Paul Hastings should not want for anything through his sister's pride.

"He was so glad to hear you were improving," she went on, "and particularly said you were not to worry about the papers. It seems they have some important clue, and feel positive of recovering them."

"If they only could," sighed Paul. "To think that I should have lost them! And they meant a small fortune to the Robinsons. What if they should become poor, and through me!"

"Oh, you silly boy! Stop that nonsense this moment. There! I heard Clip coming. I am glad, for she knows better than I how to control you."

It was Clip who entered the room, but what with her buoyant, happy way, and the great bunch of flowers she carried, one could hardly be certain it was only a girl - it might have been some fairy of sunshine.

"Well!" she exclaimed, glancing from Paul to Hazel. "You are better, Paul. Has Hazel been treating you again with some of her magic suggestion business? At any rate, I cannot deny its power." She flittered over to the bed and playfully buried Paul's face in the bouquet. "There! Aren't they splendid? And you would never guess who sent them. Guess, Hazel."

"Ed," hazarded the girl.

"No, indeed. You try, Paul."

"Walter Pennington," replied Paul, smiling.

"Indeed, Walter probably has forgotten my very existence."

"Then it was -"

"Oh, you would never guess. It - was - Rob Roland!"

A dark look stole over the face of the young man on the bed. "I don't like him, Clip," he said.

"Neither do I," she replied promptly. "That is precisely why I am so nice to him. I have to keep friends with him just now. And I have not the slightest doubt his motive is identical with my own." She paused to laugh indifferently, then she tossed aside her dust coat and stood revealed in spotless white linen. "How do you like me?" she asked, straightened up to her short height. "Am I not a full-fledged `strained' nurse, now? You know I am summoned to court this afternoon, and all the papers will describe me."

Her brightness seemed infectious. Paul leaned upon his elbow, and Hazel was actually interested in Clip's new costume.

"Yes," she went on. "You see, Mrs. Salvey has been called to account for Wren - did you ever hear of anything so ridiculous? Those lawyer relatives of hers pretend to believe that Wren is being neglected because we have taken her away from the supposed care of that absurd doctor. Well, I just told Mrs. Salvey to answer the summons and go to court. It will be the best thing that ever happened to have her get her real story before the public."

"But what about yourself ?" asked Hazel. "They will ask you how old you are, and what is your occupation "

"And my friends will all fall dead." Cecilia did not appear worried at the prospect. "Well, I shall say I am not as old as some girls, and that I am engaged in being a member of the Motor Girls' Club."

"That is precisely where your trouble will begin," said Paul. "The motor girls will never stand for a 'strained' -"

"Indeed, I am not the least bit afraid that I shall lose the friendship of Cora and her brother. Even Walter and Ed will think it jolly to have kept up the joke. Of course" - and she hesitated - "some of the others -"

"Well, you can count on us," declared Paul warmly. "And if ever I get out of this trouble, and am well again, I am going to take Hazel for a long tour. You might -"

"Oh, you silly! I might go along? Where on earth would I get seventy-five cents to go to Europe with?"

She placed the bouquet on the small table near the window. "There; I guess the flowers will not contaminate us. But when he gave them to me - or, rather, sent them, there was a note in the box," she added.

Both Hazel and Paul looked their question.

"Yes," replied Clip. "Would you like to hear the note?" She took from her pocket a slip of paper. "It always strikes me as odd that people who try hardest to do one thing, and mean another, fail utterly to hide the intention. Now this gentleman, who writes with such solicitation about Wren, says he really misses seeing her, declares frankly that Jack Kimball and I were seen to smuggle her off in Jack's auto, and then - But let me read the finish. I am spoiling the effect:

"`Of course you have the child safe,'" she read, "`and no one questions your ability to care for her. All the little clandestine trips which you and your friend made to the Salvey cottage happened to have been observed.' Just hear the boy! Happened to have been observed, when I knew he was watching - saw him on more than one occasion." She turned over the page of business letter paper, and continued:

"`But the fact that I, her own cousin, am denied the privilege of seeing her makes the thing look odd.'

"Now do you see what that means?" asked the girl. "He is trying to make me feel that it would be better to produce Wren than to keep her away from the lawyers, because it looks `odd.' Well, I'll take my chances on the odds," she said with a laugh; "and Wren Salvey will be `produced' when I am sure that the motor girls' strange promise will be kept. We have those smart men just where we want them now, and if they want Wren they must give us that table."

"You think they know where the table is?" asked Hazel.

"I am not so sure of that," responded Clip, putting away the paper and preparing to place upon the center table some of the contents of her satchel. "But I do know that this man, Reed, is Mrs. Salvey's second cousin. She told me he was always interfering between Wren and the popular grandfather. Now, if the table contained the will, as Wren declares, and if that same table was sold at auction, by this man, Reed, or through his management, it seems more than likely that he could trace it."

"But if he could find it, why would he not do so, and destroy the document?" asked Paul.

"Bright boy!" declared the girl. "That only goes to show, Hazel, that when a girl gets a thought she stops. When a boy gets one he looks for another. I think now that perhaps the old table is safe in some unthought-of place, and that perhaps -"

"That is why they wanted to get the promise book, to find if any clue to its whereabouts might be within its pages," put in Hazel. "Well, I know that Cora Kimball will find that table if it is in any house around here. She vowed when she started out she would either bring back the table or acknowledge herself beaten. The latter possibility is actually beyond serious attention "

"Whew!" Paul almost whistled. "But our little sister is progressing. Talk about professions, Clip. I rather fancy there will be more than one to report at the final meeting of the Motor Girls' Club."

CHAPTER XX

AT THE MAHOGANY SHOP

It was Duncan Bennet who suggested the auto meet. The town of Breakwater had never gone beyond the annual dog show, and this progressive young man confided to his cousin Daisy that on a certain day next week he expected several of his friends from out of town, who were sure to come in autos, and:

"Why not tell them to `slick up' their machines, and you girls could do the same? Then, oh, then!" he exclaimed, "we could run a real up-to-date auto meet. I can round up fifteen machines at least. And the girls! Why, the fame of the motor girls will then be assured. You will actually have to appoint a press agent."

The cousins were strolling through the splendid gardens of Bennet Blade, as Duncan called the long, narrow strip of family property that, for years, had been famous for its splendid gardens, not flower beds, but patches of things to eat.

"I think it would be perfectly splendid," declared Daisy, her eyes full of admiration for her good-looking cousin. "And I know the girls will like it.

That settled it. Duncan Bennet went straight to his room, scribbled off a number of notes, threw himself astride his horse Mercury (called Ivy for short), and was on his way to the post-office before Daisy had time to stop the exclamation gaps in the girls' faces with the correct answers to their varied questions.

Some days lay between the proposition and the fete, and this time was to be spent on the road, as the girls had yet some miles to cover before they would turn back toward Chelton.

There was a visit to be made at a ruins in Clayton; this was an underlined note of Ray's on the itinerary. Then Maud wanted so much to see a real watering place in full swing. This was put down as Ebbinflow, and would take up at least an entire afternoon. Tillie had a craze for antiques, and there was a noted shop only twenty miles from Breakwater. So when Cora facetiously suggested that the party start out from a given point, go their separate ways and get back to Chelton for the auto meet, the girls realized that they would have to "boil down their plans" to fit the time allotted for the tour.

The trip to the Clayton ruins occupied a whole day. The girls started early and took their lunch, which Bess said would be eaten in a crumbling, moss-covered and ivy-entwined tower. The ruins fully came up to expectations, and the girls, leaving their machines at the roadside, began their explorations.

"Isn't it just perfect!" exclaimed Ray. "I wish I had my sketch book along."

"She wants to outdo Washington Irving," called Cora, poising on a tottering stone.

"Look out!" suddenly called Bess. "That stone, Cora -"

A scream from Cora interrupted her, for the stone began to roll over, and Cora only saved herself by a little jump, while the piece of masonry toppled down upon a pile of bricks and mortar.

"My! That was a narrow escape!" gasped Maud. "You might

have sprained your ankle."

"Which would have been all the more romantic," added Cora, smiling faintly. "It would have been material for Ray's sketchbook."

"Never, Cora!" cried Ray. "But come on. Let's go to some less dangerous part of this ruin. You know they say this was once a church, but was made into a sort of castle by an eccentric individual -"

"Who did dark and bloody deeds and whose spirit now haunts the place," interrupted Maud.

"Oh, don't!" begged Ray. "It's not quite as bad as that, but I heard some one say that on certain dark nights that -"

"Stop it!" commanded Cora. "My nerves are all right, but I'm still shaky from that stone. Let's see if -"

"Oh!" cried Bess suddenly. "There's something there, girls," and, with dramatic gesture, she pointed to a pile of leaves in one corner. "Something moved there, I'm sure of it!"

They looked, and all started as the leaves actually did move.

"Come on!" cried Ray. They gathered up their skirts and were hurrying from the old room into which they had penetrated when the leaves rustled still more, and from them came a tiny snake. There was a chorus of screams and Cora found herself alone in the ruined chamber. She was pale but resolute as she followed her companions sedately.

"Weren't you awfully frightened?" asked Ray as Cora joined them.

"No indeed," she answered. "I prefer a live and seeable snake to some haunting, unseeable rumor that only appears on dark nights. But let's get out into the sunlight and admire the ruins from a better perspective. Besides it's getting near lunch time."

It was more reassuring out of doors, they all admitted, and after admiring the picturesque remains of what might have been either a church or fort as far as appearances now went, they got the hampers from the cars and feasted. Then, sitting in the shade, they discussed many things until lengthening shadows warned them that it was time to go.

"Now for a jolly day to-morrow," remarked Maud as they neared their stopping place that night. "If only we have good weather."

She had her desire. Never was weather more perfect, never were better country roads discovered and never could there have been a more jolly party of girls.

Maud was enchanted with Ebbinflow. She declared the watering place was a perfect fairyland, but some of her companions hinted that it was the style of the gowns that attracted her. Still they spent the best part of a day there, enjoying the bathing and coming back in the cool of the evening much refreshed.

"Now, Bess, it's your choice for our destination to-morrow," announced Cora at a little luncheon just before retiring time. "But please don't choose ruins or a watering place."

"The woods for mine," announced Bess. "I heard of a lovely grove about twenty-five miles from here -"

"Twenty-five miles to find an ordinary grove," said Maud.

"Oh, but it's not an ordinary one," declared Bess. "It is quite extraordinary."

A delightful fancy dress ball was given that evening at the girls' club, where our friends stopped, and this made a pleasant break in the tour and a welcome relief from spark plugs, carburetors and the cranking of motors, much as the girls had come to care for their cars.

Two days more were spent in visiting well-known places of interest, and on one trip Maud and Bess, who managed to slip away from their companions, went through several old farmhouses in search of the table. Once they had hopes that they were on the track, as an elderly woman declared she had just what they were looking for, but it proved to be far from it, though she was anxious to sell it to them.

"Oh, dear, I hoped we could find it," said Bess as they came out.

Next morning Tillie declared it was her turn to say where the trip should be, and she picked out an exclusive antique shop, about twenty miles from Breakwater, in which direction the cars were soon speeding.

"I'll get a warming pan if there is one in the place," announced Tillie, whose love for the old copper pan with the long and awkward handle was almost a joke with her friends.

"Well, I do hope if you can't get a pan that you'll not load us up with lead pipe and such stuff," said Cora with a laugh. "I remember very well that last day at school when you came back from Beverly. My, what a sight you were! What did you ever do with the junk?"

"Indeed, it was not junk," objected Tillie, "but a lot of the very handsomest glass knobs and brass candlesticks, and my samovar."

"You surely did not carry a samovar!" exclaimed Maud.

"Indeed I did," replied the little German, "else I should not have gotten it in the morning. I know those antique men. They are like a thermometer - go up and down with simple possibilities."

Ray was as pretty as ever, Maude just as sweet and Daisy just as gentle, while Cora and Gertrude had added new summer tints to their coloring. Adele and Tillie were still bubbling over with enthusiasm, the twins were exceptionally happy, the morning mail having brought good news - so that all were "fine and fit" when they started on the ride to the antique shop.

The day was of that sort that comes in between summer and fall, when one time period borrows from the other with the result of making an absolutely perfect "blend."

Ray had changed places with Belle Robinson, so that Belle was in the Whirlwind and Ray in the Flyaway, and when the procession was moving it attracted the usual public attention.

But the motor girls were now accustomed to being stared at; in fact, they would have missed the attention had they been deprived of it, for it was something to have a run with all girls - and such attractive girls.

"What if we should find the table at the antique shop!" suddenly said Belle to Ray. "Somehow I have a feeling -"

"Let me right out of your machine, Bess Robinson," joked Ray. "I have had all I want of `feelings' since we started on this trip. I rather think the one where the goat or sheep or whatever it was did the actual `feeling' was about the `utmost,' as Clip would say. Poor Clip! I wonder what she is about just now."

"About as frisky as ever, I'll wager," said Belle. "I never could understand that girl."

"Well," objected Bess, "it would be hard to understand any one who is only in Chelton two months at summer. If you were at school all year and came home for new clothes, I fancy I would scarcely understand my own twin sister."

"Strange," went on Ray, "that boys always so well understand a girl of that type. Now I do not mean that in sarcasm," she hurried to add, noting the impression her remark had made, "but I have always noticed that the girls whom girls think queer boys think just right."

"Pure contrariness," declared Bess. "I don't suppose a boy like Jack Kimball thinks more of a girl just because she keeps her home surroundings so mysteriously secret."

As usual, Bess had blundered. She never could speak of Jack Kimball and Clip Thayer without "showing her teeth," as Belle expressed it.

The machines were running along with remarkable smoothness. The Flyaway seemed to be singing with the Whirlwind, while Daisy's car had ceased to grunt, thanks to the efforts of the workman at her aunt's place.

"What will the antique man think of three autos stopping at his door?" inquired Adele of Cora.

"Think? Why, it will be the best advertisement he ever had. Likely he will pay us to come again," replied Cora.

The street upon which "the mahogany shop" was situated was narrow and dingy enough - the sort of place usually chosen to add to the "old and odd" effect of the things in the dusty window.

The proprietor was outside on a feeble-looking sofa. As Cora predicted, he evidently was honored with the trio of cars that pulled up to the narrow sidewalk. Tillie, with the air of a connoisseur, stepped into the shop before the little man with the ragged whiskers had time to recover from his surprise.

"Have you a warming pan?" she inquired straightaway, whereat, as was expected, the man produced almost every other imaginable sort of old piece save, of course, that asked for.

But Tillie liked to look at all the stuff, and was already running the risk of blood poison, as Cora whispered to Gertrude, with her delving into green brasses and dirty coppers.

With the same thought uppermost in their minds, Bess, Belle and Cora were soon busy examining the old furniture. There were many curious and really valuable pieces among the collection, for this man's shop was famous for many a mile.

"Tables!" whispered Belle. "Did you ever think there were so many kinds?"

Cora approached the owner. "Have you an inlaid table - a card table or one that could be used for one? I would fancy something in unpolished wood."

"I know just what you mean," answered the man, "and I expect to have one in a few days. In fact, I already have an order for one - with anchors and oars inlaid."

Cora did not start. She winked at Bess, who was always apt to "bubble over."

"Anchors?" repeated Cora. "Set in on the sides, I suppose? Well, that would be odd. But where can you get such a piece as that?"

Cora did not mean to ask outright where the piece might be obtained; what she meant was: "That will surely be a difficult thing to find."

"Oh, there is one - some place," replied the man, little dreaming what a tumult his words were creating in the brains of the anxious motor girls. "And when I get an order I always get the article. I shall have a warming pan for this young lady by to-morrow noon."

"Then suppose I order a table, like the one with the oars and anchors?" ventured Cora. "Could I get that?"

"Oh, no, miss," and he shook his head with importance. "You do not understand the trade. That would be a duplicate, and in furniture we guarantee to give you an original - I can only get one seaman's card table, and that is ordered."

Cora smiled and walked off a little to gain time, and to think. Her manner told the girls plainly not to mention the matter. She would act as wisely as she was capable of doing. She overhauled some blue plates and selected a pair of "Baronials."

The man went into ecstasies, describing "every crack in the dishes," Maud said to Daisy, but Cora bought the plates, and paid him his price without question.

Adele and Tillie had piled up quite a heap of brass and copper, and, unlike Cora, they argued some about the cost, but finally compromised, and put the entire heap into an old Chinese basket which the man "threw in."

"Then I cannot get a table," said Cora, purposely displaying a roll of bills which she was replacing in her purse.

"Not exactly that kind," answered the man. "But something very much handsomer, I assure you. If you will call in a day or two I will show you something unmatched in all the country. A house has just sold out, and I have bought all the mahogany."

CHAPTER XXI

PERPLEXITIES

When Cecilia Thayer in her own little runabout, the Turtle, went over the road to Mrs. Salvey's cottage, after the visit to the Hastings, her alert mind was occupied with many questions.

She had advised the mother to go to court to account for her own child, a most peculiar proceeding, but one insisted upon by a well-meaning organization, the special duty of which was to care for children. What sort of story Mrs. Salvey's relative may have told to bring such a course about, neither she nor Cecilia knew. But at any rate a private hearing was arranged for, and now Cecilia was on her way to fetch the widow to town.

Driving leisurely along, for the Turtle could not be trusted to hurry, Cecilia had ample time to plan her own course of action, should the judge insist upon having Wren shown in court. This Cecilia felt sure would be dangerous to the extremely nervous condition of the child, and it was such a move she most dreaded.

"I will call Dr. Collins," thought Cecilia, "and have him state the facts, if necessary. But then I would have to give an account of my own part," came the thought, "and that would mean so much to me just now."

The "burr r-rr-r" of an approaching automobile startled her. She turned and confronted Rob Roland.

"Well," he exclaimed, his pleasure too evident, "this is luck. Were you going to Aunt Salvey's?"

Cecilia was annoyed. But she had no other course than to reply that she was going to the cottage.

"So am I," replied the young man, "and very likely our business is of the same nature."

"I am going to fetch her into town to the hearing," spoke up Cecilia, "and I have to hurry along."

"And I, too, was going to fetch her. She is quite in demand, it seems," and he stretched his thin lips over his particularly fine teeth in something like a sneer. "I wish I had known you were coming out; I should have invited you to ride with me."

"Thanks," said Cecilia indifferently. "But I could hardly have accepted. I had some calls to, make as I came along."

"Yes, I saw your machine at Hastings. How's the chap getting on?"

"Paul is almost better," replied Cecilia, making an effort to get out of talking distance. But he knew exactly why she sent her machine ahead, and while too diplomatic to actually bar her way, he, too, opened the throttle to increase the speed of his car.

It was very aggravating. Cecilia had expected to have an important talk alone with Mrs. Salvey.

Without a doubt this was also the very thing Rob Roland intended to do. If only she could get Mrs. Salvey into her car. But if she should prefer to ride with her nephew.

For some short distance Cecilia rode along without attempting conversation with the young man who was driving as close to her car as it was possible for him to do. Finally he spoke:

"Have you ever been in a courtroom?" he asked.

"No," she replied curtly.

"Then you are sure to make a hit. Bet your picture will be in the paper to-morrow."

"What!" gasped Cecilia. "I understood this was to be a private hearing."

"Nothing's private from the newspaper chaps. They make more of chamber hearings than the open affairs. Always sure to be something behind the doors, you know."

The thought flashed through the girl's mind that he was trying to frighten her - to keep her away from the hearing.

"Well, I hope they have decent cameras," she managed to say indifferently.

He glanced at her with a look that meant she would make a picture. And in this, at least, he was honest, for the girl was certainly attractive in her linen coat, her turn-over collar and her simple Panama hat. She looked almost boyish.

"Better let me call Aunt Salvey," he said as they neared the cottage. "But there she is - waiting for us."

Cecilia urged the Turtle slightly ahead, then stopped suddenly. She was almost nervous with suppressed excitement.

"All ready?" she asked as Mrs. Salvey greeted first her, then the young man.

"Yes. I wanted to be on time," replied the woman, stepping down from the porch.

"Well, you cannot ride in two cars," called young Roland, "and this is - if I must be impolite - the best machine, Aunt Salvey."

"But you had an appointment with me," pressed Cecilia, pretending to joke. "I would not trust even Mr. Roland to get you there on time, so I came myself."

"Of course," replied the widow, puzzled at the situation, "it was good of you to come, Rob, but I must go with Miss Thayer. I had arranged to do so."

"Just as you like," he said, tossing his head back defiantly, "but you know it would look better. Oh, we know perfectly well where Wren is," he sneered, "and if you go to see her this afternoon I am going, too."

So this was his scheme - he would follow them to find the child's hiding place.

Mrs. Salvey stepped into Cecilia's car. Her face was whiter than the widow's ruche she wore in her black bonnet. She trembled as Cecilia took her hand. What if she were making a mistake in trusting so much to this young girl, and so defying her antagonistic relatives! What if they should attempt to prove that she was not properly caring for her child! And if they should take Wren from her!

"Perhaps I ought not to anger him," she whispered to the girl. "Do you think I had best go with him?"

"After I have had a chance to say a word or two, you may get out if you like," replied Cecilia hastily. "But I must caution you not to mention where Wren is, no matter how they press you. If they insist upon knowing I shall call Dr. Collins. That is the most important thing. Next, don't tell who were the last persons who signed the promise book. Now, you may get out and make a joke of it. I will trust to luck for the rest."

CHAPTER XXII

THE CHILDREN'S COURT

Judge Cowles was a gentleman of what is called the "old-fashioned" type. He was always gentle, in spite of the difficult human questions he was constantly called upon to decide, and which necessarily could not always be decided to suit both parties involved in the legal dispute. But when Mrs. Salvey walked into his room and took a seat beside Cecilia Thayer he started up in surprise. He had known Mrs. Salvey long ago, when she lived by the sea with her father-in-law, Captain Salvey. Many a time had judge Cowles ridden in the little boat that the captain took such pride in demonstrating, for the boat was rigged up in an original way, and the captain was choice about his companions.

"Why, Mrs. Salvey!" he exclaimed, with the most cordial voice. "I am surprised to see you!"

Mrs. Salvey bowed, but did not trust herself to speak. She felt humiliated, wronged, and was now conscious of that deeper pang - stifled justice. Judge Cowles would be fair - and she would be brave.

Cecilia, young and inexperienced as she was, felt a glad surprise in the words of the judge; if he knew Mrs. Salvey he must know her to be a good mother.

A man of extremely nervous type, who continually rattled and fussed with the typewritten pages he held in his hand, represented the Children's Society. Evidently he had prepared quite an argument, Cecilia thought. Close to him sat Rob Roland, and the stout man whom the motor girls had met on the road after the robbery of the mailbag. Cecilia recognized him at once, and he had the audacity to bow slightly to her.

There were one or two young fellows down in the corner of the room, sitting so idly and so flagrantly unconcerned that Cecilia knew they must be newspaper men - time enough for them to show interest when anything interesting occurred.

The case just disposed of - that of a small boy who had been accused of violating the curfew law - was settled with a reprimand; and as the crestfallen little chap slouched past Cecilia, she could not resist the temptation of putting out her hand and tugging pleasantly at his coat sleeve.

"You'll be a good boy now," she said, with her most powerful smile. But the agent of the Children's Society, he with the threatening papers in his hand, called to the boy to sit down, and the tone of voice hurt Cecilia more than the insolent look turned fully upon her by Rob Roland.

The judge was ready for the next case - it was that of the Children's Society against Mrs. Salvey. Cecilia could hear the hum from the newspaper corner cease, she saw Mr. Reed, he of Roland, Reed & Company, and the same man who had just bowed to her, take some papers from his pocket.

Then the judge announced that he was ready to hear the case.

"This woman, your honor," began the nervous man, "is charged with wilfully neglecting her child in the matter of withholding the child from relatives who have for years been both supporting and rendering to the child necessary medical aid."

Mrs. Salvey's face flushed scarlet. Cecilia was almost upon her feet. But the others seemed to take the matter as the most ordinary occurrence, and seemed ,scarcely interested.

"This child," went on the agent, "is a cripple" - again Cecilia wanted to shout - "and mentally deficient."

"That is false!" cried Mrs. Salvey. "She is mentally brilliant."

"One minute, madam," said the judge gently.

"To prove that the child has hallucinations," pursued the man, reading from his papers, "I would like to state that for some years she has kept a book - called a promise book. In this she collected the names of all the persons she could induce to put them down, claiming that when the right person should sign she would recover some old, imaginary piece of furniture, which, she claimed, held the spirit of her departed grandfather."

The man stopped to smile at his own wit. Cecilia and Mrs. Salvey were too surprised to breathe - they both wanted to "swallow" every breath of air in the room at one gulp.

"And the specific charge?" asked the judge, showing some impatience.

"Well, your honor, we contend that a mother who will wilfully take such a child away from medical care, and hide her away from those who are qualified to care for her, must be criminally negligent."

The judge raised his head in that careful manner characteristic of serious thought.

"And what do you ask?" he inquired.

Cecilia thought she or Mrs. Salvey would never get a chance to speak - to deny those dreadful accusations.

"We ask, your honor," and the man's voice betrayed confidence, "that this child be turned over to the Children's Society. We will report to the court, and make any desired arrangements to satisfy the mother."

Turn Wren over to a public society! This, then, was the motive - those Rolands wanted to get the little one away from her own mother.

"Mrs. Salvey," called the judge, and the white-faced woman stood up. As she did so, Mr. Reed, the lawyer, advanced to a seat quite close to that occupied by the judge. Rob Roland shifted about with poorly - hidden anxiety.

"You have heard the charge," said the judge very slowly. "We will be pleased to hear your answer."

"One minute, your honor," interrupted Lawyer Reed. "We wish to add that on the day that our doctor had decided upon a hospital operation for the child, the child was secretly smuggled off in an automobile by a young girl, and a young sporting character of this town."

Had Cecilia Thayer ever been in a courtroom before, she might have known that lawyers resort to all sorts of tricks to confuse and even anger witnesses. But, as it was, she only felt that something had hit her - a blow that strikes the heart and threatens some dreadful thing. The next moment the blood rushed to her cheeks, relieved that pressure, and she was ready - even for such an insulting charge.

Mrs. Salvey was again called, and this time she was not interrupted. She told in a straight-forward manner of the illness of her little girl, of her own difficulty in obtaining sufficient money to have the child treated medically, and of how her husband's cousin, Wilbur Roland, senior member of the firm of Roland, Reed & Company, had come forward and offered her assistance.

"Then why," asked the judge, "did you take the child away?"

Mrs. Salvey looked at Cecilia. Lawyer Reed was on his feet and ready to interrupt, but the judge motioned him to silence.

"I took her away because I feared the treatment was not what she needed, and I had others offered," replied Mrs. Salvey.

"Other medical treatment?" asked the judge.

"Yes," answered the mother.

"Then she is being cared for?" and judge Cowles looked sharply at the children's agent.

"Most decidedly," answered Mrs. Salvey with emphasis. "And not only is she better, but can now stand - she has not been able to do that in ten years."

"It's a lie!" shouted Rob Roland, so angered as to forget himself entirely. "She is a hopeless cripple."

"Have you any witness?" asked the attorney of Mrs. Salvey, while the judge frowned at Rob and warned him to be careful or he might be fined for contempt of court.

The mother turned to Cecilia. "This young girl can corroborate my statement," she answered.

As Cecilia stood up the reporters actually left their places and very quietly glided up to seats near the trembling girl.

"Would they make a scandal of it?" she was thinking. "That lawyer's remark about Jack Kimball "

"Your name?" asked the judge.

She replied in a steady voice.

"And your occupation?"

Cecilia hesitated. She was not yet ready to make public the ambition she had so earnestly worked for.

"A student," she replied finally.

"Of what?" asked Rob Roland.

"Young man," said the judge sternly, "I am hearing this case, and any further discourtesy from you will be considered as contempt."

The youth smiled ironically. He was already accustomed to such usage, and did not mind it in the least if only he could gain his point, but this time he had failed.

"You know the child - Wren Salvey?" asked the judge.

"Yes. I have been in close attendance upon her for some weeks," replied Cecilia.

"And you can state that she is improved in health since leaving her mother's house?"

"Very much improved. If she had not lost a very dear treasure, over which she grieves, I believe she would be almost well soon."

Cecilia looked very young and very pretty. She spoke with the conviction of candor that counts so much to honest minds, and judge Cowles encouraged her with a most pleasant manner. The newspaper men were scribbling notes rapidly. Rob Roland was looking steadily at the chandelier at the risk of injury to his neck - so awkward was his position.

"You are the young lady who removed the child?" questioned the magistrate.

"Yes," replied Cecilia.

"And her accomplice?" shouted Rob Roland questioningly.

"Leave the room!" ordered the judge. "I think there is a different case behind this than the one we are hearing. I shall inquire into it, and, for the good of the child and her wronged mother, I shall order a thorough investigation. What motive have those who brought up this alleged case? There is absolutely no grounds for this action. The case is dismissed."

So suddenly did the relief come to Cecilia that she almost collapsed. She looked at Mrs. Salvey, who was pressing her handkerchief to her eyes.

"It is all right," whispered Cecilia. "Oh, I am so glad!"

A stir in the room attracted their attention. Cecilia turned and faced Jack Kimball.

Jack was hurrying up to the judge's chair, and scarcely stopped to greet Cecilia.

"Mr. Robinson wishes you to detain these gentlemen a few minutes," said Jack to judge Cowles. "He is on his way here."

A messenger was sent to the corridor after Rob Roland. The other lawyers were discussing some papers, and in no hurry to leave.

Presently Mr. Robinson and two other gentlemen entered. The face of the twins' father was flushed, and he was plainly much excited.

"I have just heard from my daughters," he began, "who are away on a motor tour. They state that the day my papers were taken from the mailbag they met on the road a man answering the description of this gentleman," indicating Mr. Reed. "They described him exactly, his disfigured thumb being easily remembered. Now the young fellow who was `held-up' that day, and who has been sick since in consequence, also says he felt, while blindfolded, that same one-jointed thumb. Further than that," and Mr. Robinson was actually panting for breath, "my girls can state, and prove, that this same man was at a tea-house near Breakwater discussing papers, which the young girls who conduct the tea-house plainly saw. The papers were stamped with the seals of my patent lawyers."

Rob Roland was clutching the back of the seat he stood near. The lawyer accused, Mr. Reed, had turned a sickly pallor.

Jack Kimball stepped up. "There is present," he said, "one of the motor girls who was on the road at that time. She may be able to identify this man."

What followed was always like a dream to Clip - for, leaving off legalities, we may again call her by that significant name. She faced the man to whom she had talked on the road, he who had wanted to help her with her runabout when she was unable to manage it herself. It was directly after Paul Hastings left them, and within a short time of the happening which had meant so much to Hazel's brother. Clip told this, and, strange to say, the lawyer made no attempt to deny any part of her statement.

"We are prepared to answer when the case is called," he said. "But it seems to me, Robinson, you went a long way for detectives. Did not the motor girls also tell you that they met me on the road to Breakwater two days ago?"

"Judge, I demand those papers!" called Mr. Robinson. "This fellow does not deny he took them."

"When the ladies leave the room," said the judge quietly, with that courteous manner that made Clip want to run up to him and throw her arms about his neck, "we may discuss this further. We are indebted to the young motor girl for her identification."

When Clip took Mrs, Salvey out they went directly to the Kimball home, nor were they now afraid of being followed by the threatening and insulting Rob Roland.

CHAPTER XXIII

THE MOTOR GIRLS ON THE WATCH

Cora Kimball was turning away from the antique shop as indifferently as if nothing there interested her. The other girls looked at her aghast.

Bess could scarcely be motioned to silence, for the "little mahogany man" came to close the door of the tonneau, incidentally to look over his customers.

"If you come again in a day or so," he said to Cora, "I will have tables," and he rolled his eyes as if the tables were to come from no less a place than heaven itself. "Oh, such tables!"

"I may," replied Cora vaguely. "But I fancy I may have a seaman's table made. I would not be particular about an original."

"Wait, wait!" exclaimed the man. "If you do not care for an original I could make a copy. The one I am to get is something very, very original, and I will have it here. There is no law against making one like it."

"Well," said Cora, "I will be in Breakwater for a few days, and I may call in again. There," as he handed in her blue plates, "these are splendid. Mother has a collection of Baronials."

Then they started off.

Bess drove up to the Whirlwind.

"Why in the world didn't you ask who had ordered the table?" she almost gasped. "If you knew that you could easily have traced it."

"Wait, wait!" exclaimed Cora, in tones so like those of the shop proprietor that the girls all laughed heartily. "I will go to the shop again, and then I will see. Perhaps I will get the original - and then - well, wait - just wait."

"You are a natural born clue hunter!" declared Daisy, "and I am just dying to get back to Aunt May's to tell Duncan."

"Now see here, girls," called Cora very seriously, so that all in- the different machines might hear her, "this is a matter that must not be mentioned to any one. It would spoil all my plans if the merest hint leaked out. Now remember!" and Cora spoke with unusual firmness; "I must have absolute secrecy."

Every girl of them promised. What is dearer to the real girl than a real secret - when the keeping of it involves further delights in its development?

Once back at Bennet Blade the girls whispered and whispered, until Cora declared they would all, forsooth, be attacked with laryngitis, if they did not cease "hissing," and she called upon Doctor Bennet to bear out her statement.

Duncan was going to Chelton, and of course he took the trouble to ask what he might do there for the Chelton girls.

What he might do? Was there anything he might not do? The Robinson girls declared that their mail had not been forwarded, and they could not trust to mails, anyhow, since their father's papers had been lost. Would it be too much trouble for him just to call? To tell their mother what a perfectly delightful time they were having, and so on.

And Maud Morris hated to bother him, but could he just stop at Clearman's and get her magazine? She was reading a serial, and simply could not sleep nights waiting for the last instalment.

Of course he would go to see his uncle, Dr. Bennet, Sr. In fact, it was with Dr. Bennet he had the appointment; and when Daisy started to entrust him with her messages to her father, he insisted that she write them down - no normal brain could hold such a list, he declared.

Ray was what Bess termed "foxy." She did not ask him to do a single thing. "She thinks he will fetch her a box of candy, or a bottle of perfume. That's Ray," declared Bess to Belle.

Cora certainly wanted to send many messages, with the opportunity of having them go first-hand. It did seem such a long time since she had seen Jack; then there was Hazel, poor child, penned up with a sick brother. And Wren and Clip. Why couldn't Cora just run in to Chelton herself with Duncan?

The thought was all-conquering. It swayed every other impulse in Cora's generous nature. Why should she stop at the thought of propriety? Was it not all right for her to ride with Doctor Bennet, to reach Chelton by noon and return before night?

She must go. She would go if every motor girl went along with her.

Mrs. Bennet was one of those dear women who seem to take girls right to her heart. As I have said, she was small and rosy, with that never-fading bloom that sometimes accompanies the rosy-cheeked, curly-headed girl far into her womanhood. Cora would go directly to her, and tell her. She would abide by her judgment.

Mrs. Bennet simply said yes, of course. And then she added that Cora might start off without letting the girls know anything about it. That would save a lot of explanation.

How Cora's heart did thump! Duncan was going in his machine, and, like all doctors, he always preferred to have a man drive - his chauffeur was most skilful - doctors, even when young in their profession, do not willingly risk being stalled.

But in spite of Cora's one guiding rule - "When you make up your mind stick to it" - she had many misgivings between that evening when her plans were made, and the next morning when she was to start off with Duncan Bennet. The other girls had gone out to an evening play in Forest Park, one of the real attractions of Breakwater, and at the last moment Cora excused herself upon some available pretense so that she was able to get her things together and see that her machine was safely put up, and then be ready to start off in the morning before the other girls had time to realize she was going.

"It does seem," she reflected, "that I am always getting runaway rides." Then she recalled how Sid Wilcox actually did run away with her once, as related in the "Motor Girls." "And," she told herself, "I seem to like running away with boys."

This was exactly what worried Cora; she knew that others would be apt to make this remark. "But I cannot help it this time," she sighed. "I have to go to Chelton, or -"

Cora was looking very pretty. Excitement seems to put the match to the flickering taper of beauty, hidden behind the self-control of healthy maidenhood. Her cheeks were aflame and her eyes sparkled so like Jack's when he was sure of winning a hard contest.

"Dear old Jack!" she thought. "Won't he be surprised to see me! That will be the best part of it. They will all be so surprised."

She went down to the study, where she was sure to

find Duncan.

"I suppose your mother has told you of my mad impulse," she began rather awkwardly. "Do you think the folks will be glad to see me?"

What a stupid remark! She had no more idea of saying that than of saying: "Do you think it will snow?" But, somehow, when he put up his book and looked at her so seriously, she could not help blundering.

"They ought to be," he said simply. Then she saw that he was preoccupied - scarcely aware that she was present.

"I beg your pardon," he said directly, "but I was very busy thinking, just then."

"Oh, I should not have disturbed you," she faltered. "I will go away at once. I just wanted to be sure that you would wait for me - not run off and leave me."

"Oh, do sit down," he urged. "My brain is stiff, and I've got to quit for to-night. I haven't told you what takes me to Chelton - in fact, I haven't told mother. You see, she thinks I am such a baby that I find it better not to let her know when I am on a case. But the fact is, I am just baby enough to want to tell some one."

He arranged the cushions in the big willow chair, and Cora sat down quite obediently. She liked Duncan - there was something akin to bravery behind his careless manner. "What he wouldn't do for a friend!" she thought.

"Your case?" asked Cora. "I am very ignorant on medical matters, but I should love to hear about the Chelton case. I fancy I know every one in Chelton."

"Well, you know Uncle Bennet, Daisy's father, is quite a surgeon, and he has been called in this case by Dr. Collins. It is a remarkable case, and he has asked me to come in also."

"It is that of a child who has been a cripple for some years, and who now is making such progress under the physical-training system that she promises to be cured entirely.

"A child?" asked Cora, her heart fluttering.

"Yes; and I rather suspect that you know her." He seemed about to laugh. "Uncle mentioned your brother's name in his invitation for me to go in on the case."

"Oh, tell me," begged Cora, "is it Wren?"

"Just let me see," and he looked over some letters. "It seems to me it was some such fantastical name - yes, here it is. Her name is Wren Salvey."

"Oh, my little Wren! And Clip is doing all this! Oh, I must go! Is she going to be operated upon?"

"Seems to me, little girl," and the young doctor put his hand over hers as would an elderly physician, "that you are over excitable. I will have to be giving you a sedative if you do not at once quiet down. The child is not to be operated upon, as I understand it. It is simply what we call an observation case."

"But she is at our house - she has been there since I came away. Why, however can all that be going on at home and no one there but the housekeeper -"

"The child was at your house, but is now in a private sanitarium," he said quickly. "I have had the pleasure of being in close correspondence with your friend Clip."

CHAPTER XXIV

CORA 'S RESOLVE

For a moment Cora was dumfounded. Duncan Bennet a close friend of Clip!

The next moment the riddle was solved.

"Why, of course you know Clip," she said. "She goes to your college."

"Yes," and he ran his white fingers through his "fractious" hair. "The fact is, Cora, I am quite as anxious to see Clip as to go in on the case. Haven't seen her since school closed."

"I'll likely have some trouble in finding her," he added presently. "Never can find her when I particularly want to, but if she is in Chelton I'm going to hunt her up."

"Won't she be at the sanitarium?" asked Cora, and she wondered why her own voice sounded so strained.

"I think not," he replied. "Clip is a poster-girl, in our parlance, and we don't let them in on real cases."

"Poster?" asked Cora.

"Yes; it means she has had her picture in the college paper, with `Next' under it. I don't mind saying that I cut out that particular picture."

"It must be lots of fun to be in such affairs," said Cora. "I have often thought that the simple life of society is a mere bubble compared to what goes on where girls think."

"Well, I am going early," he said pleasantly. "I suppose you don't mind running away before breakfast."

"No, indeed," she answered. "I rather fancy the idea. If I ever trusted myself to meet the girls I would surely `default.'"

"All right. My man is always on time. Mother will see that we are not hungry - I've got the greatest mother in the world for looking after meals."

Cora laughed, and arose to go.

"I've told you a lot," he said rather awkwardly, "but somehow I felt like telling you."

"You may trust me," replied Cora lightly. "I have such a lot of secrets, that I just know how to manage them - they are filed away, you know, each in its place."

"Thanks," he said. "You know, we don't, as a rule, speak about our professional friends. Don't say anything to Daisy about Clip. I think she would die if she knew I fancied her."

He said this just like a girl, imitating Daisy.

"Why, she likes Clip," declared Cora. "We all do."

"Wait," he said, and he raised a prophetic finger, "wait until Clip sails under her own colors. Then take note of her friends. This is the thorn in her side, as it were. She speaks of it often."

How Cora's head throbbed! Perhaps, as Duncan had said, she was over excited. But just now there seemed so many things to think about.

If she went to Chelton she might hear something that would give her a clue to Wren's book. Jack insinuated that he had a clue when he spoke to her over the 'phone. What if she should be able to trace both the book and the table! And bring Wren into her own!

As if divining a change in the girl's mind, Duncan Bennet said:

"Now, you won't disappoint me? I am counting on your company."

"Well, I shall have to dream over it," replied Cora. "Mother says it is always safest to let our ambitions cool overnight."

"`Think not ambition wise, because 'tis brave?'" he quoted. But he did not guess how well that quotation fitted Cora's case.

It seemed scarcely any time before the girls were back from the park, just bubbling over in girlish enthusiasm about the wonderful woodland performance. And that Cora should have missed it! Even Gertrude, the staid and steady, could not understand it.

The Bennets' home was a very large country house, but with all the motor girls scattered over it the house seemed comparatively small. Chocolate and knickknacks were always served before bedtime, and Daisy had reason to be proud of her part in the entertainment of the girls.

"And to-morrow," said Adele, between mouthfuls of morsels, "we shall have to decorate for the fete. I am going to do the Whirlwind all my own way, am I not, Cora?"

"You certainly may," replied Cora vaguely. "I am the poorest hand at decorating. I prefer driving."

And they all wondered why she took so little interest in the preparations for the fete.

"I know," whispered Bess. "You are thinking of that little mahogany man. And so am I. I can't just wait to see the table."

Bright and early, the next morning the girls were astir. They had need to be "up with the lark," for the gathering of stuffs with which to decorate cars is quite a task, and they planned to make the fete a memorable affair, as Belle put it.

"Wait till Cora comes down," said Tillie. "Won't she be surprised that I have already been over the meadow, and gotten so many beautiful, tall grasses!"

Mrs. Bennet appeared at that moment.

"My dears," she began, "I have a surprise for you. Cora has taken a run home - she really had to go, but she will be back by nightfall. Now, there," to Daisy, "you must not pout. Cora has been a faithful little captain, and, from what I understand, there have been a great many things to demand her attention at home. Go right on with your plans, and make her car the very prettiest, and when she gets back she will have some reason to be proud of her allies. I have arranged to be at home all day, and to do whatever I can to assist you, in Cora's place."

The girls were utterly surprised, but what could they say? Show displeasure to so affable a hostess? Never!

What they thought was, of course, a matter of their own personal business.

CHAPTER XXV

A WILD RUN'

"Speed her up, Tom," ordered Dr. Duncan Bennet to his chauffeur, as he and Cora started out that bright, beautiful morning. "We will have all we can do to cover the ground and make home by nightfall."

"Without a single stop," remarked Cora, "I calculated we could do it. Do you think there is any possibility of us failing to get back?"

"Tom knows no end of short cuts," said Duncan, settling himself down comfortably. "We take quite a different route to that which you girls came over."

"Oh, yes, of course. We could never get to Chelton and back in one day over the roads which we came by," replied Cora.

"The one controlling thought is," said the young physician, "that an automobile is not a camel. No telling when its thirst will demand impossible quenching. But this is a first-rate car," he went on, "and it has never gone back on me yet."

"It rides beautifully," agreed Cora, as the machine was speeding over the roads like the very wind. "After all, I do believe that an experienced chauffeur is a positive luxury "

"Now, now!" exclaimed Duncan. "Don't go back on your

constitution. You will have to report, I suppose. What do you imagine our little girls are thinking and doing about now?"

Cora laughed. Duncan seemed amused at the idea of "stealing" the captain of the club - he liked nothing better than a "row" with girls.

"Well, I suppose," said Cora cautiously, "that they are scouring Breakwater for things to decorate the machines with. I am glad that I entrusted the Whirlwind to Tillie - she is so artistically practical that she will be sure to avoid making holes in the car to stick bouquets in."

"The fellows will be up to-night. They have taken rooms at the Beacon. There'll be no end of a rumpus if they strike Breakwater, and I am not there to pilot them."

"Likely our girls would attempt to put them to rights," said Cora, joking. "Just fancy a crowd of students, and those silly girls."

"It is well that they can't hear you," remarked Duncan. "Of course, you are very - very sensible."

"You mean - I should not have come?" she said, her face flushing.

"Oh, indeed, I meant nothing of the sort," he hurried to explain. "In fact, I never could have carried out my plan if you had not come along. I am going to bring Clip out for the meet."

"Oh, wouldn't that be splendid!" exclaimed Cora. "If only we can manage it. But she is always so busy -"

"Then I intend to make her stop work for a few days at least. I want my brother to meet her, and this - well, quite an opportunity."

Cora looked at the earnest young man beside her. "Clip is worth knowing," she said simply. Then she added: "I wonder if we could arrange it to have Hazel come? It would be just glorious to have the club complete after all our little drawbacks. If her brother is better I will not take `no' for an answer. I shall simply insist upon Hazel coming."

Cora was aglow with the prospects - if only everything would go along smoothly and no other "drawback" should occur.

"Your friends are from Exmouth, aren't they?" asked Duncan. "I ought to know some of them; we played their team last year."

"Oh, do you know Ed Foster? And Walter Pennington?" asked Cora.

"I happen to remember their names," said Duncan. "I would be glad if we could manage to have them come out to the show. Let me see. How could we fix it up?"

"Jack has a car, and so has Walter," replied Cora, while the chauffeur looked at his speedometer and noted that they were doing twenty-five miles an hour.

"Then," said Duncan, "if we can fix it - But that observation case will take quite a little time."

"You can attend to your case, and get Clip," said Cora with a mischievous smile, "and I will attend to the boys."

"Oh, my!" exclaimed Duncan. "You are ready and willing to make the `round up.' Well," and the car gave an unexpected bump that almost threw Cora over into her companion's arms, "I would like first rate to have them all come to Breakwater, and our fellows would count it the best part of their vacation to have an auto run of that kind. If we find everything all right out in Chelton we will call a special meeting of the motor girls, the girls being you, and the motor boys being me, and then we will come to the quickest decision on record."

Cora was arranging her goggles and veil. The speed of the car was playing sad havoc with her costume, and she was not too independent to want to look well when she got into her home-town.

"Look out, Tom!" called Duncan to his man. "Here is about where they enforce the speed laws, isn't it?"

"We have to take chances," replied the man, "if we expect to cover the ground."

"Mercy!" exclaimed Cora. "Please do not take any chances with speed laws. I have a perfect horror of that sort of thing."

"What's she doing?" asked the doctor.

"Only twenty miles, sir," replied the chauffeur, "and they allow us fifteen."

"Couldn't we just as well conform to the regulation speed?" asked Cora anxiously. It was rather unusual for her to show such timidity.

"Leave it to Tom," replied the young doctor. "Chauffeurs are like house-maids - they must not be interfered with."

Up to this time Cora had really not noticed the speed. Her conversation with Duncan had been altogether engrossing. But now she began to appreciate the situation, and this precluded all other considerations, even the thoughts of Chelton.

Duncan Bennet had no sister, and, consequently, was not versed in the art of "fidgets." He only knew the ailment when it took definite form. But Cora was getting it - in fact, she now felt positively nervous.

How that machine did go! The speed delighted Duncan. Tom

was like an eagle bending over his prey - he urged the car on with such determination. Once or twice Cora felt bound to exclaim, but Duncan only shook his head. It was going, that was all he seemed to care for. Near the station they were obliged to slow up some to look for trains. As they did so Cora saw another car dash by, and in she recognized the man now known to her as Mr. Reed, Rob Roland's cousin.

She made no remark to Duncan; he seemed so occupied with his own thoughts. But when, after a few minutes, the same car passed them again, having made a circuit on a crossroad, and the same man stared at Cora as if to make sure it was she, she felt a queer uneasiness.

This time the other car shot ahead at such a wild pace that even Duncan's machine was not speeding compared with that.

"Talk about going!" commented the physician; "just look at that fellow. If he can use up that much gasoline and escape the law, no need for us to worry."

The chauffeur was simply intent upon speed - he seemed to have gone speed crazy, Cora thought.

They were traveling over a perfectly straight road, and Duncan Bennet took out his field glasses.

"Here," he said to Cora, "I often find these interesting when on a long journey. Take a peek."

Cora adjusted the glasses and peered ahead.

"That man," she said, "has stopped at a small shed -"

"That's the constable's hang-out," remarked Duncan. "I had to stop there once - just once," and the thought was evidently funny, for he laughed boyishly.

"Yes," went on Cora, "there is some one talking to him. Oh,

Duncan," and she clutched his arm nervously, "do tell Tom to drive slowly past there, for I think I know that man."

"Go slow, Tom," called Duncan carelessly. "We might be held up. Just let me take the glasses, Cora."

He peered through the strong lenses. "The other car has gone on," he said. "Perhaps the cop is a friend of your friend's"; and again he laughed, much to Cora's discomfort.

On and on the machine flew. Finally they were within a few rods of the little shed by the roadside. A man on a motor-cycle was waiting. As the Bennet car came up he shot out into the center of the road.

Duncan did not mistake his intention. Tom turned his head and gave the other a meaning look. Then the chauffeur slowed down - slower and slower.

"Stop!" called the man on the motor-cycle, at the same moment dismounting from his wheel.

Tom almost stopped. Cora thought he had turned off the gasoline, but the next moment he had shot past the surprised officer, and was going at a madder pace than ever.

Cora was frightened. Some motor-cycles can beat ordinary automobiles; she knew that. But Duncan was laughing. If only that man, Reed, was not on the same road just then.

"Can you make it?" asked Duncan, calling into the chauffeur's ear.

"Don't know," replied the man. "But we may as well get as far out of the woods as possible."

"Don't worry, little girl," said Duncan to Cora with that self-confidence peculiar to those who are accustomed to being obeyed. "We are all right. It is only a fine, at any rate, and I always carry small change."

"Stop!" yelled the man at the rear. "You cannot cross the line, and if you don't stop soon you will find your tires winded."

A revolver shot sounded.

Tom drew up instantly. "I don't fancy putting on new tires," he said coolly, "so we may as well surrender."

Duncan looked at the officer in a perfectly friendly way.

"Well, what's up?" he asked indifferently.

"You ought to know," replied the man, scowling angrily. "If I hadn't stopped you land knows but you would have been over the falls. What's the matter with you fellows, anyhow? Can't you take a joy ride without committing murder and suicide ?"

"You're mistaken," replied Duncan. "I'm a doctor on a hurry call -"

"Yes, you are ! You look it!" and the officer sneered at Cora. "Tell that to the marines!"

"Well, what's the price?" demanded Duncan with some impatience. "I'm in a hurry."

"Wait till your hurry cools off," said the officer, who from his own wild chase was now plainly uncomfortably warm. "You made the marked-off distance in the shortest time on record, from post to post in one minute."

"How do you know?" asked the chauffeur sharply.

"What's that to you?" replied the officer. "Didn't I see you?"

"You did not!" shouted Tom. "Some one `squealed,' and you have no proof of what you are saying."

The man hesitated. Then he blurted out: "Well, what if a friend did tip me off? Wasn't he in as much danger from your runaway machine as the next one?"

"That man!" whispered Cora to Duncan. "He stopped and told him to arrest us."

"Well, the price?" called Duncan, with his hand in his pocket. "I tell you I am a doctor, and I am in a hurry to get to Chelton. Can't you make it something reasonable - and then something for your own trouble?"

The man eyed Duncan sharply. "I was told you would say just that," he said with a curious laugh.

"And that is just what the other fellow said to you," spoke Tom. "Now look here, Hanna. I know how much you have got out of this already, and I happen to know the sort of coin that that sneak, Reed, carries. He has offered me some - at times. He travels out here quite some of late. Take my advice and be square. It is all bound to come out in the wash."

Cora gazed at Duncan in astonishment. "I told you," said the latter, "that it is best to leave a good man alone. Like a good cook, they usually know their own business."

But the officer was not so sure. He hesitated, then said: "Well, I see judge Brown over in the meadow. He can settle it. Come along."

CHAPTER XXVI

LEGAL STRATEGY

Cora was in despair. To be thus detained when there was not an hour to spare! Tom drew the machine well to the roadside. Duncan leisurely climbed out and then asked the girl if she would remain in the car.

"That's the mean part of this business," remarked Duncan; "they don't want money - they want time - good, honest time."

Then, of a sudden, with that boyishness that Cora had so greatly admired in so thoughtful a young man, he sprang off on a run toward the meadow, where the constable had indicated the judge could be found.

"Come on, friend," he called good-naturedly to the officer on the wheel. "When a thing's to be done, may as well do it. The sooner the quicker," he joked, while Cora wondered more and more how so wronged a person could be so good-humored.

Tom fussed about the machine, looking to see that the official bullet had not struck through a tire. Evidently the constable did not expect Duncan to take him at his word, and go after the squire, for it took him some time to put his wheel against a tree and prepare to follow on foot.

"You can't go that way," he shouted to Duncan. "That's

all swamp."

"Won't hurt me," replied the irrepressible Duncan. "I am taking the water cure."

Soon Duncan was talking to the farmer - and the constable was still "picking his steps" toward the spot where the two stood.

"I am sure Duncan will win him," thought Cora, "and perhaps we will not be so long delayed, after all."

But Tom could not stand the suspense. He asked Cora if she would mind being left alone for a few minutes, and soon he, too, was hurrying over the meadow.

Cora had great faith in Tom's judgment now, and was rather glad that he had gone to Duncan's help. She stepped out of the car to gather a few wild flowers, and was just about to step in again when the rumble of an approaching machine attracted her attention.

She turned and saw coming toward her that man Reed. With assumed indifference she stepped back to the road to get another flower. This took her just a bit farther from his path than she would have been in the car, but as he came up she heard him slacken, then stop.

Her heart seemed to stand still. In an instant she realized what it meant for a girl to be alone on a road - she should not have left Breakwater, and the doctor and Tom should not have left her.

"Miss Kimball," called a voice from the other car. "I am sorry to see you in this predicament. I am Mr. Reed, of Roland, Reed & Company," and he said this with all possible courtesy. "I believe we have met before, and I came back to see if I might be of any assistance to you. This speeding business is rather troublesome, and I ventured to guess that you are most anxious to be in Chelton to-day, as there are so many interesting things going on there."

For an instant Cora felt that she had wronged this man. Perhaps, after all, he was a perfect gentleman, and had nothing to do with their being detained. If only Duncan or Tom was there!

"Yes, I am in a hurry to get home," admitted Cora. "But I think we will soon be off again."

"Not very likely," went on the other. "That old judge seems to delight in keeping folks away from their business. He has the most roundabout way possible of transacting matters. I was about to suggest that if you really are anxious to get to Chelton I would go over there and speak with your friend, and, as we are not so far away from the home town, it might be wise for you to ride with me. It is very awkward for a lady to be in this position. Sometimes a newspaper fellow comes along, and, as they say, `gets a story' out of it."

"Oh, I thank you very much," she said hurriedly and not without showing her confusion, "but I will wait until Dr. Bennet comes. I am sure he will not be detained long. They should have some consideration for physicians."

"Dr. Bennet? Oh, I see. He is in a hurry, too, to get to Chelton." (If Cora could have seen the flash that shot through the lawyer's brain at that moment.) "Well, of course, he ought to be allowed to go - although we all have to keep within the speed limit."

"They are coming now," said Cora joyously, for the interview was anything but pleasant. "I will tell Dr. Bennet of your kindness "

The man cranked up instantly, excusing his haste with a glance at his watch. "Well," he said, "I have a noon appointment, so I may as well hurry on. Good morning, Miss Kimball. I suppose we shall see each other again in Chelton, as we both are interested, I believe, in the same affair - finding the promise book and finding the lost table."

Then he was off.

Duncan, Tom and the two officers were up to the car before Cora had quite recovered herself.

"That was Reed, miss, wasn't it?" asked Tom sharply.

"Yes," replied Cora.

"Well, he's a cool one," went on Tom, while Duncan looked after the receding car. "Do you know him, if I may ask?"

"Yes, and no," said Cora nervously, for the constable and justice were looking at her with some impertinence.

"I thought so. His usual game. He makes himself known. Now see here," said Tom, in a manner that made Cora think of Paul - perhaps Tom loved machines as did Paul, and was more than an ordinary chauffeur - "that man is a keen lawyer, Dr. Bennet, and he has some purpose in delaying you."

"Delaying me!" echoed Duncan.

"No," interrupted Cora. "It is in me he seems to have the interest, for he asked me to ride back to Chelton with him. Oh, I know!" she exclaimed. "It is in Wren! He is the lawyer who has to do with Mrs. Salvey's case, and he is trying to keep Dr. Bennet away from Chelton to-day. He must have heard that you were on the case," declared Cora, as the whole strange proceeding seemed to flash before her excited mind.

"That's bad!" groaned Duncan.

The officials were talking at one side of the road.

"Look here, squire," called Tom, "this is all a putup game. You have no proof that we were going faster than the law allows. That sneak Reed simply told you so. Now own up, Hanna. Am I not right?"

"He sure said so," grumbled Hanna.

"And you had only his word?" asked the old justice angrily.

"I saw the smoke from that car, and -"

"Well, I'm goin' to let you go," asserted the judge. "I don't like this here kind of business, Hanna, and I want you after this to have all your charges first hand. Don't take no tips from nobody, d'ye hear?"

Hanna smiled. He had his hand in his pocket, and it may as well be told that there was also in the pocket something which resigned him to letting the automobilists go. Reed had attended to the compensation.

"Just as you say, judge," remarked the constable.

Duncan put his hand out to the old squire. "Here, squire," he said. "I do this openly. I want you to take this, not as a bribe, but as a personal gift, which I have a perfect right to offer you. You are doing me a kindness, and also this young lady a kindness, and the one most concerned is a helpless little creature who waits until I reach Chelton to know whether or not she is to be made perfectly well, so to speak. Not that I am the one to say that, but because a noted specialist will wait for all the other doctors. It's a long stony, but I will let you know how we make out if I beat that sharper into Chelton."

Cora couldn't speak. She, too, put out her hand to the old squire, who was wiping his eyes and shaking his head against Duncan's gift. Finally the young doctor prevailed upon him, and then once more they started on their mad run for Chelton

CHAPTER XXVII

AGAINST THE LAW

Two hours later Cora almost fell into the arms of her brother - so overstrained were her nerves after the exciting ride.

"Oh, Jack," she exclaimed, "I had the awfullest time! It is very well to be a girl and imitate boys in the matter of risking; but I say, Jack, it is always risky."

"Well, I am glad you have found that out, little girl," answered the brother, putting her comfortably down in the big armchair. "What's the particular risk now? No more stolen girls?"

"Oh, that was your part," she said, laughing. "And, by the way, I hear you are quite a successful kidnaper."

"Not so bad. But you should have seen the time we had to get Wren to the sanitarium. She didn't want to leave here, and had a mortal fear of a hospital. But how are you?" and he looked into her flushed face. "I declare it seems moons since I've seen you."

"And all the other planets since I saw you, Jack. I wonder will I ever have the courage to tell you all about it?"

"Wouldn't the courage just naturally come on my side? I would have to listen -"

"Oh, no. You don't have to -"

"There you go! Home ten minutes and picking a fight -"

"Jack Kimball!"

"Cora Kimball!"

Then they both laughed. It was jolly even to play at quarreling, and be real brother and sister again.

"Well, I have so little time, Jack, I must be serious. You know we have to get back to Breakwater to-night. We are to fetch you, and Ed and Walter and Clip - "

"Oh, you don't say! In a suit case or a la hamper? Ed is literally cut up about all the girls being out of town at once. He would fit in the shirt box, I fancy. But Wallie - he seems to have expanded. I doubt if you could manage him -"

"Oh, you ridiculous boy! Come on. Run after me while I get through the house. I must see dear old Margaret. How is she treating you?"

"First-rate, for Margaret. She only starved me out of the midnight rations twice -"

"You should not eat after ten, Jack. But come along. I must look over the place, and talk at the same time," and with that intention Cora started on her tour of home inspection, while Jack made all the noise he possibly could make (which was not a little), running through the house after her.

Margaret, of course, knew what the tumult was about. She always declared that boys went to college to learn how to make unearthly noises.

Cora found little out of place. Margaret was an old and trusted servant, and, in the absence of her mistress, could always be depended upon to look after the "children."

"And now I must go and get the folks together," remarked Cora. "Can you come, Jack?"

"And help you pick up the humans? Well, guess I may as well, as I am to be in the collection. But what is it all about?"

In a girl's way Cora told of the plans for the auto fete, and of Dr. Bennet wishing to have the Chelton boys meet his student friends.

"First rate!" responded Jack, when Cora paused for breath. "I rather fancy the idea of going after some of the girls. I cannot help but agree with Ed that all the girls should not leave town at once - you should take turns."

"But how about Clip? The others imagine that she makes up for quite a number - with you and Walter."

"There you go again, picking a fight," and he laughed honestly. "Now, Cora, Clip is just Clip, no more and not one whit less, but she has been so busy - oh, so tremendously busy!" He was getting into his motor togs, and Cora was already equipped for her ride about Chelton. "Say, sis," he added, "did I tell you I have my suspicions about the loss of Wren's book? Did she describe to you the pair who last signed the contract?"

"No," answered Cora, now fully interested.

"Well, she told me it was a fellow with bent shoulders, and a girl with red hair. Now, who does that fit?"

Cora thought for a moment. Then her face showed quicker than her words that she guessed who might answer those descriptions.

"Sid Wilcox and Ida Giles!" she exclaimed. "But what motive

could they have?"

"Sid Wilcox and Rob Roland are termed the Heavenly Twins, they are so often together. Now, Rob Roland has been the paragraph and the period, so to speak, in this story," said Jack meaningly.

"But why should Ida stoop to such a thing?"

"Didn't you run over her dining-car one day early this summer?" Jack reminded her. "Or was it Bess? No matter just who, it was one of the motor girls. And, besides, you did not ask her to go on the run."

"If I thought Ida Giles knew anything about that book I would go directly to her house and demand an explanation," said Cora, flushing. "Ida is too apt to be influenced by Sid Wilcox. I thought she had seen enough of the consequences of such folly."

"Oh, Ida is ambitious in that line," replied the cool, deliberate Jack.

"Well, let us start," suggested Cora. "I have quite some ground to cover. Dr. Bennet has agreed to find and fetch Clip."

"Has, eh? Smart fellow, Doc Bennet! I tried all afternoon yesterday to locate the lithersome Clip. Took a coy little jaunt of two miles afoot - some one said she had a friend out Bentley way, but I did not locate her. Hope Doc has better luck."

Jack said this in a way that opposed his words to their own meaning. He evidently meant he hoped Dr. Bennet would not have better luck.

"I am so anxious about the report on Wren," commented Cora, as they finally started off in Jack's runabout. "It will mean so much to her mother, and to her, of course."

"Well, if Clip has had any influence, I should say Wren would turn out an artist's model, physically. Clip has just about lived with the child since you went away. Of course, we had Miss Brown, and if she isn't Brown by nature as well as by name. I wouldn't say so. I never got one single smile to cut across her map."

"Shall we look for Ed first?" and Cora could not control a most provoking flush that threatened her cheeks.

"Just as you say, lady. But I have not told you - let the last moment be the hardest. Ed has taken to the ram. He is training the ram. Can't get him away from the ram. Mary's little lamb is a `bucking bronco' to it."

"Oh, I have been wondering about that," said Cora. "I thought I was to wear the ram's fleece as a sort of real baby-lamb coat next winter."

"Nothing of the sort, girl. Ed's ramifications are the talk of the town. He is to give an exhibition at college when we get back. A clear case of the lamb and Mary's school days."

"Well, where shall we hope to find him?" and she glanced at her watch. "I must find some one soon."

"Come along. I'll hunt him up. He is likely at this very moment giving Minus his morning ablutions. He called the ram Minus because the animal takes away so much of his time. Joke, eh ?"

Jack directed his machine toward the same little creek that figured in my first story of the motor girls, when Ed rescued them from a sorry plight, the Whirlwind having run into a mudhole.

"Now, I'll bet we find him by the brookside with Minus chewing daisies and, incidentally, Ed's stray clothing," declared Jack.

Along the way people appeared surprised to see Cora, and their greetings were a mixture of query and astonishment.

"There's Ida!" suddenly exclaimed Jack. "Don't let on you see her. I don't want to stop here to talk to her."

"Why?" asked Cora curiously.

"Because in about one minute you will see her trailer, the insufferable Sid, and I am not in Sid's humor.

"I would like to speak with Ida," objected Cora. "I really wanted to ask her something."

"Save it," commanded the ungovernable brother. "A thing like that gets better with time."

So they passed along, Cora having to be content with a bow and a smile to Ida Giles, who returned both promptly.

"Jack," said Cora, when they were also up to the hill behind which they hoped to find the idler by the brook, "do you know I think I have an actual clue to Wren's table. An antique man out Breakwater way has an order for one. I am watching that order."

"That's easy. When you know that Reed has been in and out of the place for some days. That's the best of being a girl. You can trace around after the most important clues and no one would ever suspect you of knowing what you are after. Now, I rather think when the fete is `pulled off,' if I may use the term," and he laughed his apology, "then there will be some doin's. I just want to see rocky Rob rumpled."

"Let us not delay talking long with Ed," proposed Cora, "for I must be at Hazel's at one - I am so anxious about Paul."

"About Paul? Why, he's all right. He's out and has been to the office," was the brother's surprising answer. "Didn't you hear about Mr. Robinson wanting to send him away for his health? Robinson has taken a great fancy to Paul. The stolen document business is also near a climax. I had a fine time trying to keep Clip's name out of the paper, the day they had the hearing about Wren. You see, I - the great first person - ran into the courtroom just as the judge was dismissing the absurd case set up against Mrs. Salvey. Of course, that was nothing more or less than a trick to get information for the other side. Well, Mr. Robinson was hurrying to court and he has passed his running days creditably, I believe when he met me. I took up his run at a moment's notice, reached the courtroom, waved my hands wildly in the air -"

"Oh, Jack!" interrupted Cora; "don't be so absurd. You know I am just dying to hear what happened."

"Then don't die until you do hear," and he slowed up at the hill. "The fact is, I just caught the whole City News force red-handed with a great story about Clip. The reporters had called her the modern Clara, and all that, but I got it away from them. I know one of the best of them, and he agreed, so they all had to. It was a good little story, for the lawyers were matched against a motor girl. That made it interesting from a newspaper viewpoint. Hello! Didn't I tell you? Say, there, Mr. Foster! Chain up the ram, Ed. We want to approach."

Just as they rounded the hill, Ed could plainly be seen as Jack had foretold - idling by the brook with the ram in the same picture, but at a polite distance from its owner.

"I thought Walter wanted the ram," remarked Cora as they neared the spot where Ed was "getting himself together."

"Oh, he did. But do you remember what the man said about having to put his overcoat on to feed that animal? Well, he wouldn't even stand ,for Walter, with or without the ulster. He tried his best raincoat and all, but the ram just went for him. But look how he purrs around Ed - tame as a kitten."

"I am not going to trust him, though," decided Cora. "One experience with Mr. Minus is enough for me. Shout to Ed to come over. I must hurry."

Cora's invitation to go to Breakwater came almost as a shock, Ed declared, but coming from Cora he would accept. Consequently he hurried the ram to its quarters, and, agreeing to look up Walter, the girl was left to pay her visit to Hazel.

"We fellows will start from here about daybreak," Jack decided, "and we will reach Breakwater about ten o'clock. That's the time Doc Bennet gave me for the official gun to go off."

It happened that Ed knew the young doctor slightly, so that he took Jack's urgent "appeal" as coming from the actual host.

"I told you he would be glad to join the Motor Girls' Club," remarked Jack, while Ed was exchanging civilities with Cora. "He's just been pining around here like a lost -"

"Now, Jack, be square," interrupted the handsome young man, whom Cora thought had actually grown handsomer in the days since she had last seen him. "I never pine. I growl - just plain growl."

"You take me over to Hazel's, Jack?" asked Cora. "Then you may go along and help look for Walter. I must meet Dr. Bennet at two-thirty. And then, I wonder, will we be able to get back to Breakwater by six."

She was thinking of her experience coming out to Chelton; also she kept on the lookout for Mr. Reed. He had hinted that there were interesting things developing in Chelton just then. He had said openly that his interest and Cora's were mutual. Would he again molest her?

With this thought she determined not to get too far away from Jack. She would have him call at the Hastings' house for her.

And the Roland, Reed & Company lawyers knew that Cora Kimball was a leader among the motor girls the club that had avowed its purpose of finding the book, as well as the table.

All this was complicated and involved, but to the shrewd lawyers, Cora knew the working out of the details was merely a matter of opportunity.

Having failed to prove Wren a subject for some "shut-in" institution, these same lawyers were now engaged on another scheme, that of trying to show that the child was detained against her will, and was actually in the possession of Cora Kimball.

Jack had told Cora all this, trying to make it a matter of small importance, and laughing at Rob Roland's initial performance, as Jack put it; but Cora felt that it was no laughing matter, and that at least the happiness of two persons - Mrs. Salvey and her delicate little daughter - was involved.

Cora and Jack were on the road, and Jack had cranked up. Ed, having made the ram secure in the field, was about to walk to his own lodgings. Suddenly a flash of red swept across the streak of brown highway. Cora recognized it instantly as Dr. Bennet's car.

He was coming at such a pace that in drawing up the gears and brakes of his machine protested with unpleasant, grinding sounds.

Dr. Bennet seemed flushed and excited. He began, without any preliminaries, to tell Cora that she must get into his car, and hurry back to Breakwater.

"I have been on the wildest hunt," he said, smiling an acknowledgment to Cora's introduction to Ed, and bowing to Jack, whom he had met earlier in the day. "I have been all over Chelton, but of course did not expect to locate you out here."

Duncan Bennet possessed that manner which is at once persuasive and at the same time courteous combination of the doctor and the man.

"You see," he continued, "I happened to overhear that you are to be subpoenaed in that Robinson patent case. In fact, I heard Reed say he would have you in an hour, so I determined to beat him back home - get you over the State line before he can serve the papers. Now, you had best jump right in. Clip is waiting for us at Wiltons'. We will pick her up and then fly."

"Oh!" gasped Cora, seizing at Jack's arm. "I am not going to run away. I will stay right at home - with my brother." Cora was as near crying as any young lady with the reputation of strength of character might safely venture. But Jack knew more of the case than he had confided to her, and he instantly agreed with Dr. Bennet.

"Run along, sis," he advised, with the jollity that makes a brave boy ever a girl's hero. "I'll be after you with the others, and it will be no end of fun. Clip's going, and I'll try to have Paul and Hazel join - if Paul is fit. Then with Ed and Walter - Say, we will have the time of our young lives! Get in with Dr. Bennet, and I'll turn back and stop in front of the ice cream place. Of course, Reed or Roland will come along that way, and of course you will be inside eating frapped subpoenas."

Cora was now climbing in beside Dr. Bennet.

"And that is why that horrid man tried to get me to ride in town with him!" cried Cora. "He wanted to make me take those papers -"

"Certainly," interrupted Duncan. "But we have fooled him thus far. Be sure to come to the show, boys," this to Ed and Jack. "My crowd will be out there to-night, but I suppose we will not see the Chelton throng until to-morrow. Excuse haste - and a bad pen," he added, laughing, while Tom gave a signal on the horn. "This is the time we make a run against the law."

CHAPTER XXVIII

CONFIDENCES

"Now, Tom," called Duncan Bennet to his chauffeur, after Clip had joined Cora, "you had better slow up some. The young ladies may want to find out whether or not they still wear hats." They had ridden fast and far.

"Oh!" exclaimed Clip, "I never had such a delightful ride. I suppose that is what you call being motor mad - going and going until you cannot go fast enough. They say it is a disease, isn't it, doctor?"

"I believe it is so defined," answered Duncan with mock dignity. "But we are not to talk disease, if you please, young lady," and he smiled a command which might easily be interpreted to mean: "You must rest from that sort of thing for a while."

Cora turned to look back over the dusty road. Her face, usually alive to every mood, was strangely set - as if too anxious to venture a change of expression. Duncan from the front seat saw her look.

"Oh, he is not coming," he said. "No need to worry now. We are across the State line."

"I never was so frightened in my life," admitted Cora. "Not that I was afraid of going to court, but I was mortally afraid we would not be able to make the run in time. I should have known better, however, for Tom had qualified before to-day."

"Tom knows just how fast this machine ought to go," added Duncan. "I don't mind Tom hearing it, either."

The chauffeur smiled in acknowledgment to the compliment. It had been a hard run, and the Chelton lawyer had only turned back at the last mile post.

"Wonder where that motor-cycle officer is now?" remarked Cora. "I mean Constable Hanna."

"Oh, he's out having a good time on what he earned this morning," answered Duncan. "One hold-up in a day is plenty for Hanna."

"I have scarcely had a chance to speak to you, Clip," Cora began, as her nervousness vanished. "I am so glad to see you."

"Well, you have been looking whole vocabularies at me, Cora, in many and various languages," said Clip in her own inimitable way. "I have been wondering whether you had turned into a Sphynx or just Liberty."

"But, Clip, I did have a fright. Suppose I should have had to give up the run, and go to that stuffy old courtroom!"

"Well, I am glad you didn't," answered Clip sincerely. "I do think that a courtroom is about the meanest place I have ever visited - and I have been in a lot of queer places. And the girls," went on Clip. "Whatever will they say to you two runaways?"

"What won't they say?" replied Duncan. "I am not to blame, of course. Miss Cora simply inveigled me into allowing her to ride with me -"

"I saw Reed pass over the back country road a moment ago,

interrupted Tom. "I might guess where he is going."

"Where?" asked the trio in a breath.

"To that junk shop on the turnpike," replied Tom. "He seems to think the shop is haunted with a valuable ghost. He goes out there almost daily."

"You mean the antique shop?" asked Cora. "Oh, I know. He is after a table. I am sure it is he who has given the order -" She stopped - her finger on her lip. Tom seemed to know so much - what if he should know about the missing table? "Have you any idea what he is after?" asked Cora directly.

"Well, I ought to know," replied Tom, "for he has made no secret of it. He has searched every attic from Breakwater to Moreland. I caught an old junk dealer in our barn the other morning, and while I watched him get down the road I saw Reed come along. Of course, he had hired the man to search where he himself could not go. He is after some sort of ancient rustic table, I believe."

Clip and Cora exchanged meaning looks. Cora had not for a moment forgotten about the antique man's promise to have the original table in a few days. She was to see this and then -

"We are not out of the woods yet," remarked Clip. "I am thinking, Duncan, that you have undertaken a large contract. You have positively agreed to have me back in Chelton by to-morrow afternoon at four o'clock."

"Oh, we will see about that," replied the physician with a sly look at Cora. "There is a telephone in Breakwater -"

"Duncan Bennet! If I thought I should be late for the `clearing-up' to-morrow I would start right now," declared Clip most emphatically.

"Oh, you won't be. We will fix it so the `clearing-up' will be late for you. I suppose you think everything that ever happened is going to repeat itself to-morrow afternoon, just because one Miss Cecilia Thayer is going -"

"Hush, Duncan! Cora does not know one word about it. She may have guessed, but that is not knowing, is it, Cora?"

"I confess to a keen curiosity," answered Cora, "but as a matter of fact I expect to be very much busy myself to-morrow. Just now I cannot see how it is all going to be managed."

"Well, when the Chelton boys arrive I guess the girls will not be so particular about their time," said Duncan. "I fancy even the captain will have to show somebody the beauties of Breakwater. But hark! Wasn't that Daisy? I just heard a breath. We are only about ten miles from home - Daisy can easily breathe that long when she is excited. Oh, I am just aching to hear what they will say, Cora," and he laughed. "I'll wager Ray will be the aggrieved one. She will likely manage to keep out of the work, don't you think so?"

Cora did not reply in so many words, but she looked acquiescence. Certainly those who knew Ray appreciated her ability to take care of her own personal self at the risk of all other matters. But Cora was thinking of something else - of Wren and the medical report. She knew better than to ask Duncan outright what might have been the result of their inquiry. Nevertheless, she could not refrain from "begging the question."

"Is little Wren happy?" she asked, without apology for the sudden turn in their conversation.

"Well, just now," replied Duncan very seriously, "she can scarcely be expected to realize either happiness or unhappiness, for we had to give her a powerful anesthetic."

"For an operation?" Cora could not refrain from asking. Clip showed no curiosity, and Cora knew at once that she was acquainted with the circumstances.

"Something of that kind," answered Duncan vaguely. "But put your mind at rest - the child has every chance of ultimate recovery. The trouble was the wrong treatment. We use purely physical training for that sort of thing."

"Could the neglect have been intentional?" asked Cora further. She had in mind the "quack" doctor so long sent to Salveys' by the Roland branch of the family.

"Oh, I wouldn't like to venture an opinion on that," replied Duncan, "but ignorance is closely allied to criminal negligence."

Clip set her deep dark eyes in a tense, strained expression. Then they all fell to thinking, and for a time conversation ceased.

"Ten more telegraph poles and we run into Breakwater," announced Duncan, while Tom eyed his speedometer. "Then for our reception!"

It seemed but two minutes, at most, from that announcement that Duncan's machine turned into the Bennet estate.

CHAPTER XXIX

MERRY MOTOR MAIDS

The runaways were forgiven, finally, although between four "enraged" young medical students, and the sextette of motor girls, Cora and Duncan had some difficulty in making it perfectly clear that the trip to Chelton was entirely unavoidable. It was a merry party that gathered in Mrs. Bennet's long drawing-room that evening to make arrangements for the run over Breakwater roads in the morning. The girls at first refused to allow Cora a sight of the decorated cars until they should be in line, but Tillie was so proud of her achievement with the Whirlwind that all finally consented, and directly after tea the cars in the garage and in the big barn were admired and inspected. Certainly the machines did credit to the fair decorators. The Whirlwind was transformed into a moving garden, the sides being first wound with strong twine, and into this were thrust all sorts of flowers in great, loose bunches. Only the softest foliage, in branches, was utilized, as Tillie felt responsible for the luster of the "piano" polish, for which the Whirlwind was remarkable. The top of the car was like a roof garden, the effect being quite simply managed, for Tillie was resourceful. She had stretched across the roof of the car a strong sheet of pasteboard. Into this she placed a great variety of wild flowers, banking the stalks, which stood into holes made in the board, with soft grasses and such ferns as might be depended upon not to "slink" in the sun.

"Wonderful!" exclaimed Cora with unfeigned delight. "But what an awful lot of trouble, Tillie!"

"It is for you," said the German girl sincerely, "and you have gone to an awful lot of trouble for me. Besides," she added, "you will look so queenly in that throne of flowers."

The compliment was rather overwhelming - especially as the strange young men were there, they with Duncan adding a new line of adjectives to the admiration party.

"You may look at our car, Cora," assented Bess, "although you were so indifferent, going away without even offering a suggestion as to what we might do."

"As if I could anticipate Belle's talent," said Cora with a laugh. "I feel I ought to answer to `which hand' when I open my eyes on her creation."

"Oh-h-h-h!"

The boys all joined in with Cora and Clip in the expressions of delight, for there was the pretty little runabout, the Flyaway, made into a "live pond lily."

"However did you do it?" asked Cora, actually amazed at the charming effect.

"I shouldn't tell," replied Belle, who was looking very pretty - at least one of the strange boys thought so. It was Phil MacVicker who "kept track" of Belle, and it was the same gallant Phil, who, late in the afternoon, helped Belle to finish up her pond lily.

"We may all guess why Belle chose that design," said Daisy, who was waiting for the newcomers to pass judgment on her own runabout. "A pond lily has a yellow head, and Belle's is just about that shade."

It would be pretty to see a yellow head in the white peals of the improvised lily. Cora satisfied her curiosity by finding out that these petals were nothing more than barrel staves covered with crushed white paper.

"You have had an awful lot to do, girls," she said with genuine sincerity. "I am actually sorry I could not have been here to help."

"Of course, mine is not so elegant," remarked Daisy, who led the way to the other carriage house, where her machine was kept, "but I fancy people will look at it."

Duncan "went wild" when he beheld what Daisy had rigged up. A veritable circus wagon - a cage, in which Daisy declared she was going to sit with whip in hand, and Nero, the big St. Bernard dog, at her feet.

"We made it out of clothes poles and laths," said Daisy proudly. "I have not taken a course in manual training for naught."

Then the boys had to fix up their cars. Duncan was tired - the other boys were frisky - so he nicely suggested that they "do as they jolly pleased with his car, so long as they left room for his feet.

Of course the boys wanted something grotesque. Phil suggested that they all carry out the circus idea, and "trail" after Beauty and the Beast. This was finally agreed to, and it was Duncan's car that they turned into the calliope, actually going so far as to hire the local hurdy-gurdy man to ride in it and do the "callioping."

"It looks as if our run home would be more auspicious than the trip we made in," said Cora to one of the very nice young students, who had offered to look over her car and see that it was in good working order. "We had a dreadful time coming out here - but I suppose the girls have told you about it."

Bentley Davis, otherwise called Ben, admitted that the young ladies had spoken of the trip, and he presumed to predict a great
time for the auto meet.

So it went on until the boys had to go back to their hotel, and the girls, after discussing all sorts of necessary and unnecessary plans, finally consented to wait for the morrow.

Tired from their enthusiasm, as well as from muscular efforts, the girls found their eyes scarcely "locked," before the bright rays of a late summer sun knocked on the tardy lids and demanded recognition.

Was it really time to get up?

If only the wasted hours of the evening past might be tucked on to the shortened time! Most things might be lengthened that way.

But, one after the other, the girls were at last awake, and so, quicker and quicker, sped the time until horns were sounding from garage and stable and even from the roadway.

"There come the Cheltons!" called Duncan as he saw Jack's car. Then Walter's with Ed rounded the gravel driveway.

From that moment, until car after car was upon the roads of Breakwater, it was a question which made the most noise, the girls talking or the boys blowing signals on the auto horns. Hazel had come with Jack, as Paul was scarcely able for the excitement, so that, after all, the motor girls were all in the run.

What a parade!

Of course, Cora, being captain, had to lead, and from the floral folds of the Whirlwind floated the club flag in the newly adopted colors, red and white, with the gold letters, M. G. C.

(Motor Girls' Club), plainly discernible in the changing sunlight.

Every one in Breakwater had heard that there was to be an amateur motor show, but few expected it to turn out into such a fine procession.

The sound of the "calliope" was truly ludicrous. To this was soon added all sorts of noises that only street urchins know how to develop spontaneously.

Nor were the young people of Breakwater to be left out of the sport, for numbers of them possessing automobiles, fell into line, after the decorated cars, until the entire little summer place was agog with such excitement as the extreme originality of the visiting colonists usually affords.

Street after street was paraded through, auto after auto wheeled along, horns tooting, whistles screeching, boys shouting, girls cheering, until one hour of this strenuous frolic seemed enough to satisfy motor girls and motor boys; and the party went to the Beacon for luncheon precisely at noon, leaving Tom to finish the honors by stripping the cars of their trappings and making them ready for a homeward trip.

Cora, however, was persuaded to leave her machine decorated, as the flowers made a pretty picture, and the return home, after the three-days' trip, seemed more auspicious when thus heralded.

Reluctantly the adieux were made - Mrs. Bennet had been so hospitable, and the boys such good company.

Duncan found an opportunity of making Clip more intimately acquainted with his mother, for she was a woman glad to be the friend of her boy's friends, and willing to take considerable trouble to show the many little social preferences.

Cora insisted on the festivities breaking up on the scheduled time, and so did Clip. Cora wanted to get to the antique shop, and Clip wanted to get back to Chelton. So after a delay, impossible to avoid where there were so many boys and so many girls, each and all wanting something to say, some question to ask, or some message to deliver, the party finally started off on the return trip of the first regular tour of the Motor Girls' Club.

CHAPTER XXX

THE PROMISE KEPT

With Jack's and Walter's additional cars the girls were able to ride home without crowding, so that the Whirlwind carried only Cora, Clip and Gertrude - the gallantry of the Chelton young men affording Tillie and Adele a chance for a most jolly trip in the little runabouts, while Hazel rode with the twins.

Cora explained that she had an errand to do on the river road, so that she might go to the antique shop without the others.

"I think it will be best to have a chance to talk with the old man quietly," she told her companions. "I am so anxious to find out whether or not he really had Wren's table, or knows anything about it."

But scarcely had she turned into the narrow street than the surprising sight of Rob Roland's car dashed before her eyes. In it were Rob Roland and Sid Wilcox.

Seeing the festooning of the Whirlwind, the driver of the smaller car slackened up, then, seeing further who the occupants of the floral car were, Rob Roland drew up to speak to Cora.

"He has just come from the antique shop," whispered Clip, "and I am afraid we are too late, Cora."

But Cora spoke cheerily to the young men, exchanging pleasantries about the auto show, and remarking that they should have been in Breakwater to see it.

"Oh, we have had our own show this morning," said Rob triumphantly. "I guess the motor girls are not such expert detectives as they have thought themselves to be."

This seemed to be aimed directly at Clip. She only laughed merrily, however, as the Whirlwind shot out of reach of the young man's voice.

"What do you suppose he meant?" she asked Cora.

"We will soon know," replied the other. "It is about the table, of course."

They pulled up to the narrow sidewalk. Cora was not slow in leaving her car. Clip was with her on the walk directly.

As they pulled off, their gloves they stopped for a moment in front of the dingy window.

Cora drew back.

"Look!" she exclaimed. "There is Wren's promise book."

"For sale here!" gasped Clip.

"I - hope so -" faltered Cora quickening her steps into the shop.

The little bewhiskered man was rubbing his wrinkled hands in apparent satisfaction. He was in no hurry to wait on his customers.

"What is that album I see in the window?" asked Cora. "Some foreign postcard book?"

"Oh, that! No, that is not foreign. It is a sacred relic of some child saint."

"For sale?" asked Cora, her voice a-tremble.

"Oh, no! No! No!" and the man shook his head gravely. "I always keep relics - for curiosities."

"Might I look at it?" pressed the motor girl, while Clip picked up something with pretended interest.

"Oh, yes, of course. But it is only filled with names, and I got it in a deal with another sale. The party who brought it here," went on the curio dealer, "the same who bought the table gave me the book in the bargain, with the understanding that I should not sell it but keep it on exhibition. They were very particular about me not selling it."

Cora instantly guessed what this meant - a trick of Rob Roland. To show her the book! To make sure it was now useless, as the table had been made secure by him, but just to put it in that case to taunt her, when she would come, as of course he knew she would, and discover there was now absolutely no hope of ever recovering Wren's long-lost treasure.

She looked vaguely into the glass case. "So you did get the table?" she said indifferently.

"Yes, that, too," said the man. But he made no attempt to display it.

"Can't I see it? You said you would make me one like it -"

"Oh, yes. I know I did. But my customer is very particular, and I have agreed not to show it."

"Cora's heart sank. She must be shrewd now or lose what she had so long worked for.

"But you made the agreement with me first," she argued. "You promised to let me see the table, and said you would make me one to order, not like it, of course, but in the same line."

The old man shook his head. He had evidently changed his mind.

A new thought came to Cora. "Has your customer paid for the table?" she asked.

"Oh, it will be paid for - it will be paid .for," and he seemed to gloat over the words, "when it is delivered."

Then it was not yet paid for - not actually bought. Clip saw instantly what Cora was striving for, but she pretended to be interested in the locked case in which rested the much-looked-for promise book.

"How do you know it will be paid for?" hazarded Cora. "Young folks often change their minds. I suppose you have a good deposit?"

"Well, no. I wanted one, but the gentleman is gone for to cash a check -"

Cora laughed. The old man's face changed.

"If they wanted the table why did they not bring the money?" she said. "I should think it would save you trouble to sell the table directly to me - if it suits me, of course. I am going away from here, and suppose the other customer never comes back?"

Still the old man did not speak. Cora saw her advantage and took out her purse.

"How much is it?" she asked boldly.

"They will pay me fifty dollars for that table," he said dramatically.

"So will I, if it suits me," she declared. "Come, let me see it."

The old man saw the new bills in her hands,

He stepped toward the door of another room, but he put up his hand to warn her not to follow.

"I will bring it," he said in such grave tones that Clip wanted to laugh - surely this was a Shylock.

While he was within the room Cora whispered to Clip, and when the old man came out Clip was gone.

He had between his hands a small, very narrow table, like the old-time card table, with glass knob at either end, and on the long drop leaves were inlaid an anchor and crossed oars.

"That is just the size," declared Cora, while she trembled so she feared the man would detect her agitation. Then she looked it over, and under she was seeking for a hidden drawer.

"Are there drawers in it?" she asked.

"Oh, my, but yes. That is why it is worth so much. The drawers cannot all be found. It is like a safe -"

Cora was sure this was the long-lost table. Oh, if she could only induce the man to let her take it

The price, she was positive, was far beyond that offered by the other customer, but that did not matter.

"You had better let me have this," she said. "I will take it right along and save express. Then make one for the other party, if he ever comes back."

The shopkeeper shrugged his shoulders - if he only would talk, thought Cora.

Cora counted out fifty dollars. The man watched her greedily. It was twenty-five dollars more than he had bargained to sell the table for. Why should he lose so much?

"May I have it?" pressed Cora.

"Well, I never before did that but he should have left a deposit," said the man.

Quicker than the girl dreamed she could do it, Cora paid the man, actually grabbed the table herself and ran out of the shop with it and thrust it into the front of the Whirlwind among the flowers, cranked up her car and darted off.

Her face was so white that she frightened Gertrude. "Don't ask any questions, dear," she said to the latter. "I must meet Clip. She has gone for a detective."

Just around the corner came Clip, and with her an officer in plain clothes. Cora swung in to the curb.

"I have it! I have it!" she exclaimed to Clip. "Is this the officer?" she asked. "And have you told him the book was stolen?"

"Oh, don't worry about the details, miss," replied the officer. "We have that thing to do every day. These fellows take anything they can get, and that being the book of a cripple, I will take chances on getting it. You may be asked to explain fully, later."

"Oh, thank you so much!" cried Cora, almost overcome. "To think we may bring both the table and the book home to Wren!"

What followed seemed like a dream to Cora. Of course she knew that it was Rob Roland who had ordered the table and Sid Wilcox who had returned the book. As the Whirlwind passed the little hotel on the road to Chelton Cora actually brushed against Rob Roland's car - and she had the table hidden amid the flowers in the Whirlwind!

In Clip's hands was grasped the promise book - Wren should have both. Poor, afflicted little Wren!

Straight to the private sanitarium they went - these two motor girls. Miss Brown helped carry the table up to Wren's bedside.

At the sight of it Wren uttered a scream - then the shock did what medical skill often fails to do. Wren Salvey sprang out of bed, touched a spring in the table and a drawer jerked open.

"There!" she shrieked, holding up a paper. "The will!" Then she fell back - exhausted.

"The shock has done it," said Miss Brown as Clip helped put the girl on the bed and Cora looked frightened. "It has broken the knot that tied her muscles. She will be cured."

Clip stepped over to a closet, and while Cora was almost fainting from excitement Clip quietly took off her motor coat. Presently she stepped back to Cora - in the full garb of a trained nurse.

"Clip!" exclaimed Cora.

"Yes," replied the girl, "I graduate to-night. Will you be able to come?"

What more should be told? With the failure of Rob Roland to get possession of the table he lost all courage and simply admitted defeat. It was Sid Wilcox who stole the book from little Wren - just to avenge Ida Giles, whose lunch basket had been demolished by a motor girl. An odd revenge, but he thought, in some way, it would annoy the motor girls. Of course Rob Roland paid him something for doing it. But all their strategy was not equal to the ready wit of Cora Kimball and her chums. Nor was this the only time that the motor girls proved their worth in times of danger and necessity. They were active participants in other adventures, as will be related in the third volume of this series, to be called "The Motor Girls at Lookout Beach; Or, In Quest of the Runaways." How they went East in their cars, and how they unexpectedly got on, the trail of two girls who had left home under a cloud, will, I think, make a tale you will wish to peruse.

It was not long after the table and the promise book had been restored to Wren, and following her complete recovery, that the suit against Mr. Robinson was dropped. Roland, Reed & Company admitted that they had arranged to have the papers taken from the mailbag, and the government imposed a heavy fine on them for their daring crime. They had done what they did with the idea of securing information, and not with a desire to keep the papers, but the Federal authorities would accept no excuses. Later Mr. Robinson secured heavy damages from the men, the disfigured thumb of one having served Clip to identify him.

As for Wren and Mrs. Salvey, with the will in their possession, they were enabled to get control of a comfortable income, and Wren could be taken to a health resort to fully recover her strength. Sid Wilcox and Rob Roland were not prosecuted for their mean parts in the transactions, as it was desired to have as little publicity as possible.

"And to think, Clip, dear, that you were deceiving us all the while," remarked Cora several days later, when she and the Robinson twins; and a few other of the chums, were gathered in the Kimball home. "I never would have thought it of you."

"Nor I," added Belle.

"But wasn't it strange how it all came about?" suggested Bess. "It seemed like fate."

"It was fate," asserted Clip. "Fate and - Cora."

"Mostly fate, I'm afraid," declared Cora. "Of course the table being disposed of at auction was a mere accident, likely to happen anywhere. The real power, though, was little Wren. She, somehow, felt that the old will was in it, and by her talk, and through her promise book, the fact came to be known to the enemies of the family. Then Rob Roland, or some of the men who used him as a tool, conceived the idea of searching for the table. They probably had the old mahogany man act for them, and he made inquiries of auctioneers and persons who were in the habit of buying at auctions. Then we came into the game, and -"

"Yes, and then Ida and Sid Wilcox, though I'm glad Ida didn't take any part in these proceedings," observed Belle.

"So am I," said Cora softly. "Well, we managed to get ahead of Rob Roland. A little later and he would have had the table, and would have found the will. Then little Wren and her mother would never have come into their inheritance. Oh, I don't see how people can be so mean!"

"And the way they treated Paul," added Clip. "They ought to be punished for that."

"Well, I guess Paul was more harmed mentally than he was physically," said Bess. "He told me the men used him very gently. It was the papers in the bag they were after."

"I think Clip gave us the greatest surprise of all," went on Cora. "The idea of a girl keeping it secret as long as she did, that she was all ready to graduate as a trained nurse! No wonder she knew how to treat Wren. I feel that she is far above us now."

"Shall I lose my honorary membership in the Motor Girls' Club?" asked Clip as she slipped her arm around Cora and pretended to feel her pulse.

"Well, I guess not! The motor girls are proud of you!"

cried Bess.

"Of course," added Belle.

Cora said nothing, but the manner in which she put her arm around the waist of Clip was answer enough.

Horace Walpole
Horatio Alger, Jr.
Howard Pyle
Howard R. Garis
Hugh Lofting
Hugh Walpole
Humphry Ward
Ian Maclaren
Israel Abrahams
J.G.Austin
J. Henri Fabre
J. M. Barrie
J. Macdonald Oxley
J. S. Knowles
J. Storer Clouston
Jack London
Jacob Abbott
James Allen
James Lane Allen
James Andrews
James Baldwin
James DeMille
James Joyce
James Oliver Curwood
James Oppenheim
James Otis
Jane Austen
Jens Peter Jacobsen
Jerome K. Jerome
John Burroughs
John F. Kennedy
John Gay
John Glasworthy
John Habberton
John Joy Bell
John Milton
John Philip Sousa
Jonathan Swift
Joseph Carey
Joseph Conrad
Joseph Jacobs
Julian Hawthrone
Julies Vernes
Justin Huntly McCarthy
Kakuzo Okakura
Kenneth Grahame
Kate Langley Bosher
L. A. Abbot
L. T. Meade
L. Frank Baum
Laura Lee Hope
Laurence Housman
Leo Tolstoy
Leonid Andreyev
Lewis Carroll
Lilian Bell
Lloyd Osbourne
Louis Tracy
Louisa May Alcott
Lucy Fitch Perkins
Lucy Maud Montgomery
Lydia Miller Middleton
Lyndon Orr
M. H. Adams
Margaret E. Sangster
Margaret Vandercook
Maria Edgeworth
Maria Thompson Daviess
Mariano Azuela
Marion Polk Angellotti
Mark Overton
Mark Twain
Mary Austin
Mary Cole
Mary Rowlandson
Mary Wollstonecraft
Shelley
Max Beerbohm
Myra Kelly
Nathaniel Hawthrone
O. F. Walton
Oscar Wilde
Owen Johnson
P.G.Wodehouse
Paul and Mable Thorn
Paul G. Tomlinson
Paul Severing
Peter B. Kyne
Plato
R. Derby Holmes
R. L. Stevenson
Rabindranath Tagore
Rahul Alvares
Ralph Waldo Emmerson
Rene Descartes
Rex E. Beach
Richard Harding Davis
Richard Jefferies
Robert Barr
Robert Frost
Robert Gordon Anderson
Robert L. Drake
Robert Lansing
Robert Michael Ballantyne
Robert W. Chambers
Rosa Nouchette Carey
Ross Kay
Rudyard Kipling
Samuel B. Allison
Samuel Hopkins Adams
Sarah Bernhardt
Selma Lagerlof
Sherwood Anderson
Sigmund Freud
Standish O'Grady
Stanley Weyman
Stella Benson
Stephen Crane
Stewart Edward White
Stijn Streuvels
Swami Abhedananda
Swami Parmananda
T. S. Ackland
The Princess Der Ling
Thomas A. Janvier
Thomas A Kempis
Thomas Anderton
Thomas Bailey Aldrich
Thomas Bulfinch
Thomas De Quincey
Thomas H. Huxley
Thomas Hardy
Thomas More
Thornton W. Burgess
U. S. Grant
Valentine Williams
Victor Appleton
Virginia Woolf
Walter Scott
Washington Irving
Wilbur Lawton
Wilkie Collins
Willa Cather
Willard F. Baker
William Makepeace
Thackeray
William W. Walter
Winston Churchill
Yei Theodora Ozaki
Young E. Allison
Zane Grey

www.ingramcontent.com/pod-product-compliance
Lightning Source LLC
Chambersburg PA
CBHW020549310726
48979CB00008B/1151/J

* 9 7 8 1 4 2 1 8 1 4 9 0 2 *